I0761214

THE LIFE OF VIOLET

The Life of Violet

THREE EARLY STORIES

BY VIRGINIA WOOLF

TRANSCRIBED,
ANNOTATED,
AND INTRODUCED
BY URMILA SESHAGIRI

PRINCETON UNIVERSITY PRESS
PRINCETON & OXFORD

Published by Princeton University Press

41 William Street, Princeton, New Jersey 08540
99 Banbury Road, Oxford OX2 6JX

press.princeton.edu

GPSR Authorized Representative: Easy Access System Europe - Mustamäe tee 50, 10621 Tallinn, Estonia, gpsr.requests@easproject.com

ISBN 9780691263137
ISBN (e-book) 9780691263243

Library of Congress Control Number: 2025936223
British Library Cataloging-in-Publication Data is available
Editorial: Anne Savarese and Emma Wagh
Production Editorial: Terri O'Prey
Jacket Design: Katie Osborne
Production: Erin Suydam
Publicity: Alyssa Sanford and Carmen Jimenez
Copyeditor: Cathryn Slovensky

Jacket image: Raoul Dufy, *Les Cornets*, c. 1924, furnishing fabric made from woodblock on linen. Adapted from image © Victoria and Albert Museum, London.

This book has been composed in Arno

Printed in the United States of America

10 9 8 7 6 5 4

CONTENTS

FIG. 1. Violet Dickinson, 1885, age twenty. Longleat Archives 4th Marchioness Albums 4, p. 15. Image reproduced by kind permission of the Marquess of Bath, Longleat.

FIG. 2. Virginia Stephen in 1902, age twenty. Photographed by George Charles Beresford. Platinum print. © National Portrait Gallery, London.

ILLUSTRATIONS

PREFACE

READER! CAN VIRGINIA WOOLF make us burst out laughing? And does anything remain to be said about her career? A newly published work of fiction answers *yes. The Life of Violet* transports us into an astonishing world where a laughing giantess builds a magical country cottage in England and tames a silver-scaled sea monster in Japan. This three-part mock-biography illuminates a little-known literary episode in Woolf's life, a slip of time between her departure from the staid South Kensington world of her birth and her immersion in the unconventional spheres of Bloomsbury.

Woolf originally drafted the fantastical, farcical, anti-fairy tales that comprise *The Life of Violet* in 1907, and scholars have always regarded the work as a minor confection written to entertain Woolf's friends and family. But the discovery of a different version of *The Life of Violet* upends what we know about Woolf's early efforts to revolutionize English literature. A typescript archived for eighty years in Longleat House, the magnificent Wiltshire estate of the Marquess of Bath, shows us that Woolf—only twenty-six, and still seven years away from publishing her first novel—reworked her draft of *The Life of Violet* in 1908 to perfect its three interrelated stories, "Friendships Gallery," "The Magic Garden," and "A Story to Make You Sleep." The newfound Longleat House typescript fills in a space we never knew was blank, its refined stories marking Virginia Woolf's first fully realized literary experiment. These stories also reveal that the future author of *Mrs. Dalloway* and *To the Lighthouse* had a flair for slapstick comedy. No restrained wit or elegant ironies distinguish *The Life of Violet*: these pages are exuberantly, uproariously, the-cook-fell-through-the-kitchen-floor funny.

The mock-biographical tales in *The Life of Violet* are loosely—very loosely!—inspired by Mary Violet Dickinson (1865–1948; fig. 1), who was thirty-seven in 1902 when she befriended twenty-year-old Virginia (fig. 2). More than six feet tall, very wealthy, and unmarried, Violet quickly became a fixture in the young writer's world, introducing her to a wide circle of aristocratic friends and serving, in part, as a composite of the mother and the older sister Virginia had recently lost. The two friends met regularly, exchanged voluminous letters, and traveled together. Violet served as Virginia's sounding board for matters private, public, and professional during years marked by trauma as well as creative growth. Crucially, she was an insightful reader of Virginia's earliest writings and facilitated her first appearances in print in 1904.

In 1907, Virginia concocted three interrelated stories as an inside joke for her friend, never intending to publish them. She invented an outsize heroine named Violet who could defy governesses and gravity alike; she served up a barely disguised (and merrily skewered) supporting cast based on their mutual aristocratic friends. Amid flights of fancy—a snowfall of sugared almonds, laburnum trees that drop gold coins, bathtubs made of painted ostrich eggs—the stories brim with decidedly Woolfian subjects. History. Women's education. The difference between fiction and biography. Above all, the stories are about laughter, especially women's laughter, a gorgeous phenomenon that loosens repressive conventions and serves as the binding element of utopian societies. And in Virginia's talented hands, these subjects become irresistible.

How did I have the good fortune of rousing Woolf's typescript from its decades-long slumber in a Wiltshire manor house? Like all the best discoveries, this one happened entirely by accident. I had long ago read the three 1907 draft stories in the New York Public Library (NYPL), where they are catalogued in the world's largest collection of Virginia Woolf's papers as a single work called "Friendships Gallery." (That title, incidentally, was Violet Dickinson's; Woolf never titled the entire work, referring to it informally as "The Life.") Charmingly typed in violet ink, the pages of this large leatherbound item bear handwritten corrections, in pencil and ink, by Virginia as well as by Violet. The stories have never been printed alongside Woolf's better-known short fictions, such as "The Mark on the Wall" (1917) or "Kew Gardens" (1919); like most Woolf scholars, I regarded them as inconsequential early steps on Woolf's lifelong journey of biographical experiments. But in 2018, a chance email exchange revealed that the stories archived in the NYPL were not the only versions Woolf wrote, and that she took *The Life of Violet* more seriously than either biographers or literary critics have realized.

In search of an unpublished memoir that Violet had written about Woolf's childhood, I had reached out to Longleat House, just outside of Bath, where a collection of Violet Dickinson's papers is housed. Longleat's response to my inquiry caught me off guard: Yes, the archivists affirmed, they owned Violet's "Memoir of the Stephen Family," and would I also be interested in "Friendships Gallery" by Virginia Woolf?

I was bewildered. Were the archivists referring to a reproduction or facsimile of the NYPL's "Friendships Gallery"?

"No," came Longleat's astonishing reply, "we hold an original Virginia Woolf typescript called 'Friendships Gallery,' hand-corrected by the author, and we have never heard of the NYPL's item."

I wrote to Carolyn Vega, curator of the NYPL's Berg Collection, who in her turn had never heard of Longleat's item. (Nor had archivists of Woolf's papers at the University of Sussex, the British Library, and King's College, Cambridge University, all of whom believed the NYPL's "Friendships Gallery" to be the only one in existence.) Two original hand-corrected typescripts with the same title: curiouser and curiouser! What, exactly, did Longleat own? Unknown literary writings by Virginia Woolf? It was a prospect at once tantalizing and impossible.

Years passed. A sequence of obstacles—international copyright law, estate rules, the 2020 pandemic that halted travel and closed Longleat House to the public—barred my access to the mysterious new typescript. In the fall of 2022, I finally traveled to Wiltshire, and, thanks to the generosity of Emma Challinor, Longleat House archivist, retrieved the typescript from its cream-colored case. Excitement rushed through me as I saw that Woolf had indeed reworked her stories in 1908. Even a swift glance at the first paragraphs revealed a degree of polish absent in the NYPL typescript, which, it now became clear, was only a rough prelude to these aesthetically refined pieces. Turning page after page on an unforgettable October afternoon, I felt as though I were reading a new work by Virginia Woolf.

Whether you are familiar with Woolf's novels or have yet to encounter her writing, I hope the small, well-formed stories in *The Life of Violet* will please you. Their riotous plots speak to readers of all ages. And like the voice of her giantess-goddess heroine, Violet—"deep with quivering shades of red and opal colour as the petals overlap each other and melt swiftly to the heart of the naked fire within"—Woolf's budding literary gifts unfurl throughout this early biographical experiment, hinting richly at masterpieces to come.

A Note on the Edition

I transcribed the three stories that comprise *The Life of Violet* from a typescript archived in Longleat House, Wiltshire, which is a revised and professionally typed version of Woolf's first draft, archived under the title "Friendships Gallery" in the NYPL. Aside from correcting indisputable spelling errors (e.g., changing "Mam'm" to "Ma'am"), I have reproduced the page layout, language, spacing, and occasionally idiosyncratic punctuation of Woolf's revised typescript (e.g., the mother's narration in the third story ends but does not open with quotation marks). This includes incorporating the handwritten edits Woolf made on the professionally typed pages. I made three silent corrections I considered essential for consistency or syntactical clarity: on p. 7, I have added a comma after "thing," on p. 15, I have changed "breath" to "breathe," and on p. 22, I have changed "begiling" to "beginning." In keeping with accepted scholarly practice, I refer to the author as "Virginia Woolf" even though she was unmarried in 1908 and her name was still Virginia Stephen.

The explanatory notes at the end of the book provide biographical, literary, and historical context that may be helpful to contemporary readers. Readers interested in specific differences between the NYPL rough draft and the Longleat typescript should consult the textual notes.

The Life of Violet

Dramatis Personae

IN ORDER OF APPEARANCE

Lady Bath. Frances Isabella Catherine Vesey (1840–1915) married John Alexander Thynne, 4th Marquess of Bath (1831–96), and had six children, two of whom were Beatrice and Katherine (*see below*).

Lady Eleanor ("Nelly") Cecil. Eleanor Lambton Cecil (1868–1959) met and befriended Virginia Stephen through Violet Dickinson. She was a prominent, active suffragist and writer. With her husband, Lord Robert Cecil (1864–1958), a barrister and politician who was awarded the Nobel Peace Prize in 1937, Lady Nelly maintained a residence in St. John's Wood in London; the couple's country estate was Hatfield House, a seventeenth-century Jacobean manor in Hertfordshire. The Cecils had no children. A round-the-world trip Lady Nelly took with Violet Dickinson and others in 1905 inspired "A Story to Make You Sleep."

Lady Beatrice Thynne. Daughter of Frances Isabella and John Thynne, 4th Marquess of Bath, Beatrice Thynne (1867–1941) and her sister Katherine (*see below*) were members of Violet's aristocratic social circle. They were frequent guests at 22 Hyde Park Gate, the Stephen family's London home. Woolf writes of attending balls and parties with Beatrice, who never married.

Kitty Maxse. "The brilliant the sparkling" Katherine Lushington Maxse (1867–1922), as Woolf described her, was, along with her two sisters, very close to the Stephen family during Virginia's adolescence and young adulthood. Kitty married Leopold Maxse (1864–1932), the prominent conservative editor of the *National Review,* in 1890. The Maxses had no children. Kitty was a well-known society hostess before her sudden death in 1922. She is regarded as the model for Woolf's Mrs. Dalloway in the 1925 novel of the same name.

Lady Cromer. Katherine Georgiana Louisa Thynne (1865–1933), Countess of Cromer, was the second wife of the statesman and antisuffragist Evelyn Baring, 1st Earl of Cromer (1841–1916) and "Maker of Modern Egypt." They had one son, Evelyn (1903–73), who would become governor of Kenya.

Mrs. Crum. Ella Sieveking Crum (1863–1948), a painter and member of the Ipswich Fine Art Club, was married to the Coptic scholar Walter Ewing Crum (1864–1944). The couple had no children. Woolf often mocked the Crums, who were primarily Violet's friends, for what she judged as their gauche or thoughtless behavior.

1

Friendships Gallery

FORTY YEARS ago (our sincerity does her credit) a child was born in a Somersetshire Manor house. Whether she was born laughing or crying, or both at once, or whether she merely accepted the situation and made the best of it, a sincere historian, anxious to use only those words that cannot be avoided, has no means of telling.

But there never was such a child for growing.

"Nurse, bring the weighing machine," said the doctor.

"It's the foot rule you want Sir," said Nurse, "if I may make so bold."

But here the child burst out crying, so lustily that all who had charge of her agreed that she was the cleverest child, the noisiest child, and the child with the finest lungs in the Parish, and that the sooner she was christened the better.

But what can you call a child, a woman child?

Now the history of Christian names is so interesting that if I had the freedom of my mother tongue, as I have it not, for a reason to be told in the appendix, I would here expound it; I will only say that forty years ago a Christian name was a Christian name, and that if you wished your daughter to answer with credit in this world and the next you branded her with the virtues of the faith from the very beginning. So when the long baby was held over the font god-mothers and god-fathers muttered, as people do on those occasions, "Mary" and when the clergyman said "Is that all?" and smiled, as though he could tolerate a little vanity now, they added "Violet" in the bolder tones of people who are come out of church though the hush is still on them. But as the child grew and became capable of inspecting her two names, of comparing them with others, she decided that though it was good to wear Mary next your skin, it was better to show Violet outside. "Miss Violet Dickinson" then, and if it hurts you to think that Lycidas was once a matter of conjecture it hurts me still more to consider how nearly Violet was Mary, how easily Dickinson might have been Jones. Here again I would digress. But this is one of Violet's earliest sayings.

Her mother. "I wish you would learn to write Violet."

Violet. "I won't write; I'd rather talk."

Miss Violet Dickinson grew to be as tall as the tallest hollyhock in the garden before she was eight, but after all our concern is with her spiritual progress. True, her size alarmed her family; her position in the ball room, they thought, might be seriously prejudiced, and before she drove to her first dance, in the Bath Corn Exchange, she had to submit to a solemn exhortation from her Aunt, who was also her godmother.

"Mary Dickinson," began the Aunt, using as Aunts do, the least palatable expression, "remember that you are neither beautiful nor wealthy, nor, for anything I can see, in any way attractive; God in his infinite goodness has caused you to grow at least six inches higher than you should grow, and if you are not to be a Maypole of Derision you must see to it that you shine forth as a Beacon of Godliness."

The Dickinson's we must add, are a Quaker family, related to William Penn, for they were transported to America in the 18th Century for stealing silver spoons.

"Love, charity, humility, Mary, are virtues above rubies, and if you possess these you may make a good match and be a happy woman. Now my dear, here is my little gift to you," and she whipped a box from her underskirt, "and when you wear it think of IT and think of ME."

Then she hung a heavy golden cross, in truth the bars were hollow, round her niece's neck, kissed her on the forehead, and wished her a happy evening.

Mary or Violet, was by this time weeping solemn tears, like those that a dog might shed who has been beaten and does not question the justice of the whip. But the carriage was waiting and the ball was beginning, and Violet must go, if she went in the spirit of a Martyr to the Stake. Now it is recorded that her first partner was a clergyman, and her second was a Squire, and her third was a Peer (we shall move in good society, I promise you) and the Peer it was who said,

"May I ask, Violet, why you come to your first dance in a Cross?"

"Because I am so ugly John, and I must be a Beacon of Godliness if I am not a Maypole of Derision, and virtue is far above Rubies."

The tail end of one eye did certainly droop over the last syllable of rubies, but that was no reason why a Christian nobleman should begin to laugh, continue to laugh, and end by laughing with such vigour that Violet lifted up her voice and laughed too, and the result was that the cross was "hauled down" (the peer said it) its value fixed, its weight judged, its purity gauged, and it was agreed that few ornaments are really more amusing than Crosses especially when they been given you by maiden Aunts and worn at your first ball. The rest of the ball was what Violet called "Rattlin' good fun" but we are writing no novel but the essence of truth. She could not tolerate for example, the final "g" of the present participle and though when made to pick it up she could hold it in her teeth for a second, directly you looked away she had dropped it in some dark corner. In the garden of the Corn Exchange, to continue the story, the nobleman proposed the Cross should be buried; but here Violet expressed some very decided opinions how Aunts were Aunts and Crosses were Crosses, and though you might drop your "G's" in talking of them you could not bury them; and if my instinct is true the cross is still in its box, and the box is in its drawer; just as the Aunt is in her cottage, and twice a year Violet visits her.

"Violet, I wish you weren't so plain - but poor Child - -"

Lately it has been "Do you know Violet, I think you are growing shorter? and better tempered?"

The day after the ball is always used by sentimental novelists endowed with words, for an effective contrast; not only does it change the scene and relieve the strain of prolonged attention—I give away these secrets the best in my possession—but it reveals quite naturally a different side of the heroes character. And so it was with my heroine, if a living woman can be called by such a title; and the critics dispute it.

When she woke in the morning the first thing that caught her eye was that emblem of her Aunt and IT which had somehow proved so versatile the night before; but now the ugly thing was one and indivisible, and Violet felt constrained to recognise it. She took it with her to her bath, and set it in the soap dish while she sponged herself. She meditated whether she should kiss it, and laughed aloud; the breakfast bell rang and she forgot all symbols in the horrible substance—she would be late for breakfast, she had not practised, and it was the morning when Fraulein Müller came to "finish" her with a German polish. So the contrast verged almost on the melodramatic, for when Violet was depressed her face stretched, and she looked up from large drooping eyes which would spill tears if you wished it.

And this morning it was the History of England, the History of the Elizabethan age in particular, that wished it. Fraulein Müller talked of the Renaissance, the Italian influence which was somehow German, the origin of the drama. Violet could only remember that Elizabeth was a "very naughty old thing", had worn pearls on her petticoat, and someone had put down his cloak for her to step on.

"But, my dear Miss Violet, that is not history!" exclaimed Fraulein Müller. "Have you not read the course I made out for you? Have you not traced the development of the Miracle-Morality-Mystery Play into the Chronicle-History, and that into the Comedy-Tragedy, and that into the History-Comedy Tragedy-Romantico-Psychology of Shakespeare? You will never do yourself credit, Mademoiselle, in the society of Bath."

It was at this point that the whole of life became intolerable.

"Nobody will ever care for me!" cried Violet.

"Nobody will ever wish to talk to you about the Elizabethan drama," said Fraulein Müller, with an accuracy that did her credit.

"But . . . ." — Human nature is weak, or strong, which ever you choose to call it, and when the lunch bell rang Fraulein Muller was wiping her eyes and saying,

"Ah, my dear Miss Violet, I have never told any one what I have told you."

Such in short was the way in which Violet acquired her knowledge of history, literature, arithmetic, modern languages, music and humanity; and that is why each governess when she left felt that she had imparted a great deal, and that it would be necessary to go on instructing her at intervals all through her life. A time comes however, parents and guardians can tell the precise second, when book learning has yielded exactly the number of drops which, taken internally, benefit the system of a maiden; a teaspoonful in excess has been known to ruin the constitution for life; some maintain that a little external polish is no bad thing.

Violet at any rate felt considerable affection for her books when she locked them in their cases before going to London for her first season; Shakespeares pages were stamped with the affairs of the heart of Mademoiselle Bourget; Keats sang of German life in a flat on the third story; Wordsworth taught her how a plain Somersetshire girl, the daughter of an Attorney can earn her living, hem her underclothing, and keep her father's drunkenness from the knowledge of the neighbours. If you ask her to quote the Ode to Duty, at this day, which she thinks the finest modern poem, and she keeps it by her bedside, she will at once tell you the story of Miss Janet Sitwell. So her regret was quite genuine when she stood on the threshold of the schoolroom, one April day, and thought of the sunny mornings, the birds and bees among the flowers, while literature sent straight avenues branching out from all sides of the lawn till it swam as a little island on an immense ocean and she could scarcely sit on her chair for a desire to voyage there.

"How I love reading!" she exclaimed, and shut the door and jumped into the carriage which stood waiting.

Now there should be here some more tremendous division than a blank space of white paper, and I suspect that my artistic skill would have been more consummate had I thrown these first pages into the waste paper basket or enclosed them within the arms of a parenthesis. For when you are writing the life of a woman you should surely begin with her first season and leave such details as birth, parentage, education, and the first seventeen years of her life to be taken for granted. For it is the merit of the first season that, like some curiously furled flower, it folds many events and qualities and experiences into one mature blossom. Clearly no one could have a season who had not been born and who had not spent seventeen years in practising for it, but as these acquirements are completely exhibited in the ball room it is mere waste of time to say how she came by them or in what proportions they are mixed. But then this Biography is no novel but a sober chronicle; and if life will begin seventeen years before it is needed it is our task to say so valiantly and make the best of it.

Violet's first season has, no doubt, some less picturesque name ın the catalogue of the century; ıt was the year when trade was worse or better than it has ever been, when there was a blight among the mayfly; when sashes were worn, and Mr. Gladstone's ministry came in or went out or stayed where it was; but for us and for her and for many now beginning to grizzle on the top, it was Violet's first season.

"Who is that very tall young woman with the pleasant expression?" asked Lady . . . .

(I forgot to say that names can seldom be used in this narrative, for many are yet alive, in high places, and so on—I must beg my reader to believe that a blank means rather more than a full name, for it is capable of feeling if you guess it aright.)

Her ladyship waved her fan as an elephant its trunk, and indeed her position in a drawing room was so gigantic that she was allowed the liberties that monkeys, sheep and asses grant to the King of Beasts.

"That? Oh, Miss Violet Dickinson."

"Dickinson - with a "y" No? Well there have been Dickinsons with an "i" - Yes, present her."

"And so Miss Dickinson, you have an 'i'," went on the august lady.

"Two eyes I think Ma'am," said Violet fixing them both on the lady's face. Such was the comicality and at the same time the wistfulness of their expression that her Ladyship's sense of humour was tickled, and she was grateful to any one who made her laugh; "I like sneezing and I like laughing," she used to say, "but it must be natural."

"I like you, Miss Whats-your-name," she said.

"Dickinson Ma'am; and a very good name too," said Violet. "And may I tuck in your Ladyship's chemise? One pin will do it, I have one myself. Thank'ee."

"Am I straight behind," asked Lady . . . . in some agitation. "Most annoying you know. One can't trust one's maid. Now who does your hair?"

"A little creature I picked up off the streets, gave her a bath, it's astonishin' what the water was like afterwards - and converted her. We go to church, hand in hand, and she tells me I shall be damned, but she prays for me."

"Miss Dickinson," pronounced the great lady as she rose, "you must lunch with me to-morrow."

"Very sorry, but I can't" said Violet.

"Then Tuesday? - Wednesday? to meet the Prime Minister?"

"I think I could come Thursday if that suits. Thank'ee."

Any one who knows the manners of the inner circle of English society will agree that this slight but faithful conversation (there was more of it than I have quoted) is as remarkable in one way as The Ode to a Nightingale in another. In both you see the same amazing precocity, the same instant penetration to the secret heart, the same perception that truth is beauty, the same mastery over material. But Violet must be allowed the credit due to one who makes fact out of barren paradox; who proves that Duchesses are as true as nightingales.

When six months later, Lady .... (the blanks yawn like awful caverns, as though the shield once withdrawn you might see all splendours and glittering lights within) had to confess that somewhere behind her name and her tremendous front door she kept a mortal body, Violet was the first to see her after the operation. She did not like to confess to others that she was so solid a fact. Then (this should come in a footnote) Violet was present at the birth of the first grandchild, now Lord .... she went to Italy with Lady .... and by feeding her with steamed breadcrumbs for twelve hours incessantly saved her from death from the puncture of a pin, which her Ladyship had swallowed by mistake; she was in the house when the cook fell through the floor, thereby revealing the presence of an unsuspected cesspool. "Enough to give you all enteric in two whiffs," said Dr. Walker, had not Violet instantly soaked the woman in salad oil and soapsuds—"the one thing that could have saved her life"—while she directed the household to fill the chasm with vinegar and burning feather beds till the doctor came. The butcher's horse falling down the area on the same afternoon, made it necessary for her to take the man to the London hospital. He recovered, and called his first child Violus (it was a boy) after her; while Lady .... put up a window in the parish church, in which the good

Samaritan helps a Leper on to his Ass, while the beast crops Violets. The horse, unfortunately, died.

From this bald and hasty paragraph a person of discrimination will construct whole chapters which I have no time to write out. But when you think what a casual bow in a drawing room did in this instance, and there are many others, you will figure to yourself a head charged with thunders and lightnings, bent beneath the winds of heaven, so piercing in the shafts of its eyes that fires will kindle and flames long blunt among ashes shoot up beneath its compulsion. Further, you will imagine a mouth, which like flame again for my figure declares its need of ashes, curls and flickers and bursts here and there into a true rose of heat, deep with quivering shades of red and opal colour as the petals overlap each other and melt swiftly to the heart of the naked fire within. Ashes, even, glow like the clouds of dusk when it flushes them. "I too have a fire within me." "I too sing a delightful song." And "My God, I can write!" such were the sparks that spurted from Duchess and kitchen maid when Violet struck them.

Among Violet's friends there was a Costermonger and a woman who sold apples; a number of people whose names would produce no kind of effect were I to write them down, and at least half a dozen who were so profoundly investigated that the surface shell was of no more importance than that "thin jacket which grasshoppers shed in spring."

Now here again it would be possible to enter into one of those intricate labyrinths of analysis which, as modern novelists expound them, turn human hearts and brains into so many honey-combs of coral. How did Violet love her friends, how did she know them? Tell me, for example, how she thought? Why did she drop her "g's" and put in her "h's"? Was she a Christian? Describe the flight of her mind, rising like a cloud of bees, when a question was dropped into it. Did she reason or only instincticise? Where does care for others become care for oneself, and at what precise point in her relationship with ..... did she cross the boundary of unselfishness and become the most selfish of living creatures?

All these questions are legitimate, and I can only answer—she had an Irish grandmother, and the Irish grandmother was one day triumphing in the mist above Loch Ness, and clasping to her breast cloud-shapes of spiritual bridegrooms, when she fell into a pit, "a pit of rocks and sulphur and the howlin' of the damned" as she described it afterwards. "And there was a man like Elijah in his burnin' mantle" who gave her "fire to drink and the flesh of wild goats and spake to me with the voice of the wind and the rain. And it was like the voice of none other, for he did the things he spake of, and lifted me in his arms and drave me behind wild beasts, like a God, to the little house in the valley and there he married me. Och Och Ochone!"

Mr. Dickinson, a North country cotton spinner who had made a fortune by inventing a new form of spinning frame, called the Throstle, would have told the story in sober prose, and there would have been bans and wedding rings and marriage settlements above all, but no prose, as I begin to discover, can tell you how Irish mists break over Lancashire rods of steel in the brain of their descendant.

2

The Magic Garden

ON A SUMMER afternoon you might have seen, had you taken the 'bus to the Jumping Elephant, turned to the left and walked on a tender green pavement beneath the trees in the gardens of Royal Academicians, and rung the bell at No. 25 - you might have seen as beautiful a sight as any in England. There were gigantic women, lying like Greek marbles in easy chairs, draped, so that the wind bared little gleaming spaces on their shoulders, who laughed as they helped themselves to strawberries and cream as though they looked upon the vision of a jocund world; who rubbed one hand deep in the rich fur of a Chow dog, where he most liked to be rubbed; who fluted up and down the scale of human speech with a round note always, who rose and strode across the lawn, their laces foaming in the grass behind them, and shook cherry blossoms from a benignant tree upon the face of a child, who crowed thereupon and clapped his hands, as at some familiar rain of crimson butterflies. And there were other ladies like flowers strayed from the beds, anemones and strange fritillaries freaked with jet, and certain straight tulips, tawny as sunset clasped by stiff green spikes—all kinds of flowers indeed, whose voices chimed like petals floating and kissing in the air, or creaked, as fresh tulip leaves creak when rubbed together, so that you long to crush the juice out of them. This is a picture of noble English ladies at tea, as true as I can make it, and if it is not spoiling the harmony, I would further suggest that these ladies think, eat and breathe—live in short—besides existing or whatever the polite word for it is, within the pages of Burke.

I will not say how they do these things, for that would require a surgical knowledge of anatomy, neither polite nor possible; for, living as I do, in a garret with one dirty charwoman who brings me Lloyds Weekly and a bunch of kippered herrings tied by the tails like candles on Friday nights, how can I imagine the taste of the cutlets which Lady B-----th eats off silver, beneath the eyes of six flunkeys in livery? Cutlets may change their shape beneath such a radiance, and Heaven knows what exquisite nerves are stimulated and begotten by mutton eaten off silver. And as it is with mutton, so it must be with other things, with books, with pictures, with love, with life. This is a very good reason why I should not attempt to describe what I do not know - why I should continue to adore it.

But two things I do know about English aristocratic ladies, and one is that they have health, and another that they have country houses; and by health I do not mean, as we plebeians mean, a power of earning our bread and eating it, but a far subtler state than that, which only a temperature tube can rightly appreciate. A temperature I have heard one lady (Mrs. M----x----e) explain, is just as good as a sea voyage. She ran to her room and fetched what she called 'a chart,' and with her forefinger she traced her weeks journey. "Here I was down below normal, oh! it was wretched - I fancied myself lying in a muddy creek, with a gray sky, forgotten by my friends, useless - a free trader; then I took just four drops of essence of a cheese, and here you see I'm over 99. The flags flying - we're out at sea

- the Cornish sea you know, with rocks and emerald water and blue sky, and there's been a Protectionist gain and all my friends love me - O do take your temperature too! The great thing in life, I'm sure, and so is Leo," she went on as one sharing a secret of importance, "is never lose your interest in things; now when you wake in the morning and see this chart before you, (I keep it over the wash stand) you think "Gracious Heavens, I'm alive!" and then you think, "now am I more alive or less alive?" And then you take your temperature. And if you think a thing, you are that thing. Now I'm certain that all life's a matter of temperature. If Darwin had always been above normal and Chamberlain was always below - - "

It cannot be denied that Violet treated such talk with the scorn that the professional has for the amateur; her passion was for operations and drains, and after listening for ten minutes or so to Mrs M----x----e she would burst forth "I'm not a valetudinarian - whats the word? And my cottage <u>is</u> a cottage, and my widow comes from slums and can't cook". And if no one sees the connection, I am not surprised, but it would really take too much time to fish the links from the sliding waters of Irish grandmothers and education and religion in which in Violet's mind they lie submerged.

But one of the flowers in the magic garden at St. John's Wood, a tall rod of a plant with queer little tassels always quivering and austere silver leaves which prick you if you don't know the way of them, was certainly Miss Violet Dickinson. She was often there, you saw her stride across the grass to slap some mournful dowager on the back, or she pulled out her note book and wrote directions for killing green fly on roses, or the address of the only man in London who can beeswax tiles, or she undertook to interview a specialist, or gave advice on the feeding of infants, the choice of husbands, or the writing of English prose.

She, though not an aristocratic lady - stay though, she had a grandmother! - owned a country cottage. When, some pages back, I was trying to label different cycles of our century I should certainly have marked the year in which Violet bought her cottage as one of the most significant. That act of hers typifies a momentous change, which will be described one of these days by Mr. George Trevelyan in his work on "The Social Life of the Nineteenth Century". "A new spirit," he will write, breathed like the wind of a rosy dawn, from the works of George Meredith, and, stirring the dusty and arid leaves now beginning to shrivel on the stunted bushes of modern life, caused them to drop these perfectly inefficient shields, relics of a purblind aristocratic age, and to put forth whatever of youth or Spirit yet remained in them. Not much in most cases!" There he laughed, and then went on, sprinkling his page with notes, to tell us how gently born ladies took to porridge off earthenware, without stays, and how they dug in gardens, and how muscles grew on their arms, and their husbands called them "Comrade" and children in vast quantities, mostly of the male sex, were born to them, and how they toiled for human brotherhood, and the sap of life sang in their veins. The Comic Spirit laughed meanwhile. But as the most capricious of chroniclers I may select one seemingly irrelevant scene and let it stand for chapters of picturesque history. I will describe, then, how Violet was staying once at H------d, where her friend Lady R----t C-----l lived, the strange fritillary freaked with jet of the magic garden. It was summer time and had one been so minded, one might have conceived long narrative poems with English peers for the persons of Greek mythology, and English gardens and country houses for the slopes of Olympus and the Temples of Bacchus. And imagination would have had no cause to turn her head aside for all that came to her there would have painted her creatures with bright scales, and plumped their limbs.

But Violet, as it was clear to any one who saw her, sitting on the most famous terrace in Europe, with the oldest oak trees in front of her, and the smoothest turf, and behind her the finest Elizabethan grey stone, had no mind for any form of narrative poetry. She was alone and had therefore no reason to veil her discontent; she had some six volumes in her lap, to fortify her solitude, but she did not look at them; four were novels hot from the press, one was a solemn Memoir and the other was a copy of the poetical works of John Keats. I repeat, it was summer morning, and a perfectly even sheet of air shifted up and down and smoothed the landscape like some subtle painters medium. Trees and little hills and far church spires all were blunted of their sharp angles, rounded and suffused, and at the same time made of solid body. You could hear, if you listened, either the kiss of the air or the chatter of insects, and suddenly a bird came swooping in a circle, with a little soft chuckle of its own. There never was a deeper or more tranquil scene, as though the colour had been steaming upwards through solid miles before it reached the earth's surface and glowed there, and as though not one yelp or discord was contained in the whole seas of air which swam continually across the sky so fine was their texture. Fauns might be hiding behind the thick laurels, or suddenly a ring of naked maidens might burst from the grove, and run, scattering rose leaves and laughing across the turf; joining hands in a fantastic circle, with backward glances into the wood behind them, whence, in a moment, the branches cracking, tawny furry eared Fauns would leap, and the whole chase would flash across the grass, white and yellow upon its green. In truth the laurels did shelter some living creature, for Violet's listless eye grew attentive and her lips smiled, as though the landscape had suddenly come to have meaning for her. It was an old ruddy bent gardener who wheeled a creaking barrow half full of laurel shoots which he had been clipping from the bushes—a somewhat prosaic interruption you might have thought, intent on your fauns, and you might have felt constrained to fit the English peasant into the picture, his servility, his brutality, his so many shillings a week, and the percentage due to the public house, his drudge of a wife and his dozen flaxen haired children. But Violet rose to her feet, with the action of a recumbent antelope, and strode towards him, as though she had the precise place ready for him in her mind.

"Good day," she began, with a heartiness that made the bent old creature straighten himself and look at her. Yes, she was a real lady, and - what was that odd feeling she gave him? The crust of demeanour which sheltered all his natural passion and protected him from ladies and gentlemen and gave him a body wherewith to appear decently in their eyes, the crust that they both agreed to accept for the real man, since the real man was not presentable was pierced by this lady's voice and her friendly gaze. He felt excited as though something long suppressed were now rising into daylight. Freedom gleamed in his eyes while he spoke, and he waved his shears towards the house as men waved bloodstained bayonnettes once before the Bastille. His conversation I must own, was as bent and smelt as strongly of the earth, as his ancient gnarled body, nor did it deal with heroic matters. He explained the best way of treating roses, and how to lay on manure, he was dogmatic on the grafting of Pyrus Japonica, and contradicted the lady flatly without apology, on the matter of Cyrus Asiatica, remembering that he knew more than she did. In short he stood there for half an hour telling her of his wife's dyspepsia, how 'caustic is poison for tumours', how a drop warms the innards, how he would think over her words, and how if ever she came their way he would be proud to give her a cup of tea "not spirits" he said with a wink, and show her the way to treat phylloxera with paraffin. He forgot for the first time for twenty years that half hours are the property of the C---l family, and have been so "for centuries and centuries I dessay."

Violet, once indoors, got out her bible and found some very good reason there for preferring to build her own house with your own hands to living in a house built for you by others. She found a phrase for her discontent, among so much that was old and beautiful, which ended with "moth and rust" and suggested a figure to her mind of bodies crusted with precious stones, as some beetles are crusted with dry excrescences, trying painfully to scrape themselves smooth against gleaming walls of steel. It was not, you perceive, that she had no love of beauty but that - how can I explain it? - there was some illicit connection in her mind between beauty and riches, beauty and luxury, beauty and selfishness, tyranny and vice. But a mixed parentage will produce these confusions, as it produces also, by a lucky jerk of the seeds, genius, humour and virtue.

When her hosts had placed her in one of the bedrooms of the house which history had painted with all manner of beautiful figures and tones, they did not guess any more than Violet herself, that they were vexing her days and haunting her nights. She would start up, when the ancient clock tolled two with a voice that seemed to break the news as gently as possible, in a temper that, if its object had been human, you would have called one of acute irritation. All she could say was that she felt suffocated, all she could do was to throw up her window and malign certain Elizabethan bolts which caught and grated. With one hand she would have torn the glass-grey tapestries from the wall, with the other she could not but point in admiration. If one could but copy them! That was her salvation.

Instantly she lighted an extra candle and began to touch and scrutinise with envious fingers; she wrote little notes, and lay awake for hours planning where to buy, how much to pay, and all the practical activities which would somehow purge beauty of its fleshliness. She slept, nor did the sheet fret her limbs any more with its smoothness, nor did she feel, when the maid came gently with her breakfast, as one bound down by chains of air.

This was the beginning of revolution, and the question which she put with tremendous animation, to her host at lunch. "Do tell me on what system is your drainage managed?" was the first shot of an attack which threatened the whole of the Elizabethan pile. They were sitting in the long gallery watching with calm benignant eyes the daily performance of sun and earth which had been so often repeated in front of them that they could almost prompt the actors. You had the impression, until Violet spoke, of an audience such as the audience of the hills beholding an evening sky; or the long gallery was a tranquil creek where ships that had done their voyages came to anchor—and then Violet spoke.

No one could tell her how the drains were managed, for no one remembered that there were drains. And yet it stood to reason—someone went to the window and tapped the dry wall—another offered to ring for a footman, but there was a spirited feeling against this—a third said, "Yes, Miss Dickinson, in a house of this size the drainage system, you may be sure, is complicated." But all, save that one restless spirit, felt a gloomy change, as though the huge honeycomb of brick were momentarily closing in on them with a gross weight; without drains it was as a body without nerves.

"Can you tell me," she piped suddenly, "where you get your roses?"

"We get them - let me see - I could find out, I could ask - "

"James Cookson?"

"Is he a flower dealer?"

"He's a gardener My lord, aged 72, and he has been in your service thirty years, and he has two sons now in your glasshouses, and knows more about roses than any man in Hertfordshire."

And then Violet obeying some native instinct that was certainly not polite, gave such a picture drawn in coloured detail of the Cookson family, that no one could help laughing; no one had been heard to laugh so loud for twenty or thirty or forty years. That night Violet heard a tap at her door.

"Is it true Violet, what you were telling us, about old Cookson," said a plaintive lady's voice.

"Every word on my honour," said Violet, who was tracing figures on a sheet of paper, with her hair down.

"Do you know it seems to me - well don't you think Violet - it would be very nice ---- "

"To have a cottage of one's own? Yes, my good woman," cried Violet.

"With real drains, and real roses, and a place to sit out in, and one's own china, and no ancestors," continued Lady R------t. Such was the beginning of the great revolution which is making England a very different place from what it was.

Not a month after the words I have quoted were spoken, a figure, tall, spare and infinitely vigorous might have been seen as the novelists say, striding along a country road, not many miles from Welwyn. She only needed a couple of terriers at her heels, and a whip in her hand to look the part which in effect she did not play, the Squire's sporting daughter. When she came to a Gate she sprung over it, admitting herself to something known in county histories as a Copse, and then, secluded from the road, her behaviour was far more remarkable. She threw up her head and fairly snuffed the air, and strode among the trees as a general on a battle field. What there was to see except a cheerful little wood already beginning to smell of autumn it was not easy to say, but Violet's eye was charged with fire and her lips moved with decision as though she issued commands to some phantom army. Sometimes she tapped a tree and nodded her head and wrote in the perennial notebook which swings by her side, as though her path through life were full of notes; sometimes she drew mystic lines on the turf with her walking stick; sometimes she dropped on her knees and smelt the ground. How does a healthy human being differ from the nobler sorts of quadrupeds? a spectator might have asked. Here were pure animal good spirits inspired by the mere mass and pungency of earth. But little we know man-woman-or Violet kind. Within six months or perhaps a year, a religious service was being held where the wood had been, and wild beauty was reclaimed for ever to the service of the domestic virtues friendship and the Christian religion. There was a Cottage and the trees were gone -- but not all of them. Such as were left flourished like cannibals on the destruction of their fellows, drastically pruned, passionately loved by their austere mistress, serving my purpose as an allegory you will perceive. Nor can we pretend, much though we admire the satiric vein, that the rule which turned a scrubby suburban copse into a distinguished dwelling place all alive with the civilised graces of flowers and fruit, the sturdy virtue of cabbage and green pea, was altogether barbaric. On this lawn I have seen many worthy and delightful people refresh themselves; Coptic scholars digging for vegetable roots as for the roots of languages twenty times buried in Egyptian sand; distinguished authoresses matching the view with words, ladies with troubles and tempers forgetting them in a desire to have "a cottage just like yours"; hospital nurses cleansing their minds from the horrid incrustations of surgery and sickness; fashionable London "making believe" with pruning hook and knife that it loves the country, as you have seen little town bred children dig holes in a corner of the Square Garden and pretend that they are really camping out with tinned food, in the Indian jungle, and that the cats are roaring lions.

But Violet was careful that too great a strain should not be laid on the imaginations of her friends; there was a real drawing room and a real kitchen and real beds when you were tired of pretending that you could do without them. And the fauns of Welwyn, whom the rites of the Christian church dislodged, were probably no more beautiful than Lady C-----r, no more witty than Lady R------t C---l (it is rumoured that she has a pointed ear) no more passionate than Mrs C-----m, no more learned than her husband, and if you have ever seen Lady B-----e T------e in her bath, studying the effects of sunlight dripping through the leaves onto naked flesh, as the French Impressionists painted it, you would not claim any superior beauty for the yellow skin of Fauns.

It is clear I hope from the very few examples I have given, that Violet's cottage stood for a symbol of many things; and that indeed is the pitfall into which her biographer is forever pitching himself. A gross brick wall would be the outcome of a lifetime of scrupulous solicitudes and the prayer with which she crowned the building was the sum of many vows. At her knee as I have said swung a little notebook; things had a way of striking her, tremendous truths struck out from the conflicts of worlds in the most unlikely places, if indeed one place were more unlikely than another. But the truth of it is that no place was unlikely to Violet's eye, so long as she could detect a human twist in it, and it was really only upon the Acropolis, in the British museum, in the great picture galleries and concert rooms and libraries that she was horribly depressed as one forced to contemplate a corpse. But these reflections transcribed in brick and mortar made the cottage, and my pitfall is the temptation that besets me everywhere to leave these symbols unexpressed and to let my heroine hide herself behind them. Often she has whisked behind a paragraph and it was only when I had done it and set it proudly in its place in the pile raised to her honour that I discovered that she was behind and not in front, that I had made a screen and no pane of glass.

At such times you would find her digging furiously in her garden or catching brambles by the neck as some deft animals catch snakes; and she would look at you with fierce melancholy and exclaim. "Nobody wants me, but I'm very happy alone. Why should they want me? I don't know anythin'- - can't do anythin' except weed, yes I do think I can keep a garden tidy and do my accounts fairly. I'm a good sister, I tell the truth and - one other thing, Oh yes, I'm a very good judge of character. But as you say that's only one, two, three, four, five good qualities, and that's not enough to make a woman of." At this she would master a tough bramble with great spines, as though it were the symbol of some creeping vice. Indeed one chapter of her tablet note book is called "Weeding Brambles, or how to kill Caterpillars". But you had come not to discuss Violet's faults but your own virtues; you had come all the way from F----y S-----e in the parish of St. Pancras for this purpose, and it was necessary not to waste time. So with whatever skill you had you recalled her to the fact of your humanity by bleating, chuckling, groaning, or offering to pull up weeds too. Then she would stride to the house and pull forth a long arm chair which she placed under a tree whence you might see a view, which you conceived as a nice blue foreground for certain human figures. Now with any good luck the talk played freely on the most interesting and instructive of subjects, modern English prose, how it is written by women, and then, for the sake of example, how it is written by one woman, its beauties, possibilities aims and, just to round the picture, defects. Indeed I should do my heroine a horrid injustice if I allowed it to be thought that she indulged literature any further than she indulged children or husbands and wives. I could of course, with time and space, disprove all her theories, and show them to be most fallaciously compounded from a confusion of morals and aesthetics, but it would be scarcely worth my while since at the end I should have to own that she was somehow, wrongly unmistakeably, unreasonably right. But as she insisted upon certain stringent virtues in character so she condemned an art without them. "Ah, if you ever wrote a word like", and then came many distinguished names "I would - -". She would have laid the book so written on the log fire, and burnt her illusions as thin as the black films of paper with sliding red eyes in them, that went out one by one. But how she came by such decision of judgment seeing that the printed page swam before her eyes, as we have shown, in a confusion of coloured shapes, of biblical texts, of odd facts relating to cabmen in the London hospital, or the love affairs of Prime Ministers, so that she would look up from Adonais in tears and say, "That reminds me I have not given Jack his ointment." —how this was done, is and must remain, as far as I can explain it, a mystery. Nor can I attempt, the number of this page warning me that I have already attempted too much, to follow the course of those conversations with which the leaves in B-----m W-----d still murmur. There were swift contrary currents on the surface, the wind veering or meeting its own blast half way, surfaces might be ruffled, and hair blown in bewilderment, but the stream steadied itself, changing its nature you perceive at the same time, as it bored beneath the obstacles on the surface, till, in the depths, it ran a swift course, straight as an arrow, ice cold, dark as steel, beneath black precipices, sparkling blue again when it ran out into the sun. Now as it is a fact that human beings will suffer almost any kind of chill and even bruise which will convince them that they live—"See, my hand - it bleeds!" - So B---m W-----d became as fashionable and famous for its healing properties as a German Spa. It would take me at least two more chapters to write out the significance of the place in the life of the time; how vows uttered in secret came fluttering down from the eaves of the house and settled on unexpectant heads, how odd half thoughts born in the Somersetshire school room, growing by fits and starts in London drawing rooms, hospitals and streets fixed on other people and started eddies in their blood, which drove them to all kinds of unforeseen experiences, but it all goes to prove that the life of Miss Violet Dickinson is one of the most singular as well as the most prolific and least notorious that was lived in our age.

In Japan they have a story fast becoming a myth, which mothers tell good children as a treat, or sick children who cannot sleep at night. Mine of course is but the English version, and all the delicate rose pinks and silvers are rubbed off it, as a schoolboy's thumb will obliterate the wing of a Peach Blossom Moth. But this is how it goes.

3

A Story to Make You Sleep

ONCE UPON a time, my child, before you were born, a great sea monster with smooth sides gleaming like silver, swam up into the harbour and lay gasping on the sands. All the people of Tokio ran on to the top of the hill and burnt the best wheaten cakes in their houses at the shrines of their ancestors, and at that moment - behold! the monster beneath gave a great roar, and his soul left him in a thin spire of smoke, spattered with blood, of a terrible sharp smell, so that it tore the nostrils. The people kissed the earth, and the priests scattered the Sacred Rose Leaves, which you know are kept in the Inner Temple in the lacquer caskets with the silver hinges, and are used to sweeten the souls of heathens who die within the city. Then they saw that the evil spirits were leaving the monster's dead body, thousands of them, little round devils, no bigger than a chin-chin's egg[x], as black as dried peas, and were making for the city. At this your Ancestors, and mine too for all this happened many thousands of years ago, were terror stricken; they knocked the earth with their foreheads, and danced round the Sacred Pear Tree, on the topmost branch of which the High Priest sat, shaking the petals

[x] The Oriental Grebe Podicipes Oristatus.

on their heads, chanting the Law, and looking back sometimes over his shoulder to see whether the city was yet in flames. Well, they danced and they danced and they danced, till the old people were too tired to dance any more, and the children had forgotten what they were dancing about. At last the High Priest cried out "Our Prayers are heard, O my children, behold the Bald Pated Crow!" And they stopped dancing, and there above them was the oldest and the baldest and the most sacred Crow in the world, who lives in a cavern on the top of Shin-To and has never been seen by any living man, though he eats the cakes which we put out for him on Feast Days, and good children never forget to save their crumbs for him—the crow I say floated above them, and cawed twice.

Some thought that he said "Tsai gun Tsai Gun"[x] others that it was rather "Tsara Gun Tsara Gun,"[xx] others again were certain that it was nothing but "Tish Gun Tish Gun".[xxx] But whatever it was he said, and now we can never know, for as I say it is ten thousand years since he was seen, he flew on in a straight line so slowly that they could follow him, towards the city. And when they dared to look they saw that it was as it has always been, the most beautiful city in the world, and the monster lay on its side quite dead and the little black spirits were gone. The people ran quickly through the streets and so happy were they to kneel on their own praying mats again that they forgot all about the Bald Pated Crow till the moon rose and they went to pray. And then what did they see? O my child never forget your Guides be they crows or men. There was a great mountain grown in the middle of the city, and it had thousands and

[x] Follow me. Follow me.

[xx] Feed me. Feed me.

[xxx] Corresponding to the English 'Caw, Caw'.

thousands of caves in it, and at the mouth of each there burnt a flame, and on the top of the mountain among the stars, grew one tree, bare as a rod, and on top of the tree sat the Crow, the Sacred Crow of the Bald Head.

Now on every roof in the city the faithful rocked in prayer; but though they prayed as they had never prayed, their vows came raining back on them like hail, for the wings of the bird covered all the city as beneath a dish cover of tin. Then the oldest and wisest struck the gongs which we still sound to call people together, and the faithful came flocking to the market place. "Unless we can entice the Crow away," they said "all the city will become before dawn one vast mountain, and snakes will run in and out of the flaming caves that were our homes." You have seen, my child, the old Blue Barrel of Grain in which every seed is as smooth and white as a pearl, for they were plucked in the fields of Muz after the flood of milk had left them. They took handfuls of these, and the High Priest bore the Barrel and danced solemnly, chanting, through the streets, drawing ever nearer to the Mountain of the Eyes of Flame. When they had come quite near they turned and danced backwards with closed lids lest the sight of the evil place should corrupt their faith or the crow blind them with drops of steel from his eye. Then they threw over their shoulders in a fan shape, handfuls of pearl white grain, now one, now another, and they sang the songs which are also shaped like a fan. Behold! as each grain fell, one burning cave went out, until there was only a single yellow hole left in the mountain in which no doubt the prime devil lived. But the Crow still sat on the peak of the tree. Now the High Priest who bore the Blue Barrel whirled it round above his head, turning a complete circle on the tip of his toes as he did so, and the barrel spun high in the air and fell and cracked its side open on the ground. And there was the crow on top of it, though no one had seen him fly. At that very moment too the last light went out, and the Sacred Crow has never been seen again. Some say that he died of a surfeit of white grain and that his body was found next day, but they are of the impious who do not know our saying. "One feather from a Crow's tail has outlived a thousand Crowns."

Next day when the people ran to their windows (many had dreamt in the night that they were swelling into mountains, and serpents darted from the right eye to the left) they saw a wonderful sight, for the black mountain had been changed, by the magic grain, into a great Rick-Shi[x] even like that where the strangers go to-day.

It was midday, the hour of silent prayer beneath the sun, when a strange thing happened. A sound was heard like a mid-summer wind among laden barley, swish, swish, the faithful bent the lower, the faithful prayed that the serpent's tail, if this was it, might strike the roof of their enemy, and might drop silver scales on to their own heads and the heads of their mothers-in-law and kinsmen, and when they had prayed all they had to pray and they looked up and behold! The strangest sight in the world! Never was the like of it seen before or since—I can but tell you what my mother told me and her mother told her. Here were two figures like nothing so much as Idols that had stepped out of the temple, draped in long garments, one of them nine or ten or twenty feet high, and the other the height of a well grown cherry tree. Whether they had tails nobody could say; they had great brown hoofs, and they made a noise as they walked, not like our speech, but like the noise that clappers made shaken by boys in the rice fields to scare crows, and now and then there was a scale of bells,

[x] House of the Homeless or Wandering People, corresponding to our 'Hotel'.

beginning high and running all the way down, as an opossum with an ivory tail comes down stairs. They had large eyes, like eggs, filled with fire to the brim, great teeth, much fur like hair, which had built a kind of birds nest on the top of their heads, where strange fruits grew and glossy leaves. They did not walk as we do, one foot before the other, but gave long springs, now this side and now that, like a puma cat. But the strangest thing of all was that instead of feeling a cold shudder in the marrow bones and exorcising it with prayers our ancestors could do nothing but laugh. One small boy indeed who had been crossed by a pelican in his cradle, threw a pebble at the Giant, to see whether he could start a crane, so he said afterwards; at any rate the pebble turned to a rose when it fell. At this miracle our ancestors should certainly have done worship, but nobody knew whom to worship, and there was danger that if they offered prayer to the wrong God, the right God would immediately devour them. This has happened many times. They did nothing then but sit in the streets and roll this side and that grinning as widely as they could, which worship evidently pleased the Monsters for the High One clapped its jaws as fast as it could like ivory castanets, and the wild Cherry tree shook her blossoms and chimed as though each pink flower was a silver bell. They were just considering what offering could be laid on the ground before them, when a Rim Shi-Ki[x] came running all out of breath and bade them make way for the Two Sacred Princesses. Daughters of Emperors were they, and came sailing over the sea on the back of a whale; one was of the nature of a Giantess, he said, who had swallowed a magic seed when she was born so that nothing on earth could stop her growing, but as her clothes grew too, it did not matter; moreover her powers

[x] Interpreter.

were as marvellous as her height, she could heal cripples, make small children appear out of bags, marriages were made by her, she could tame wild beasts, and make surly bears dance; she was forever in motion because the seed within her was forever putting forth shoots. She was worshipped in her own land where there were Temples raised to her, and maidens brought offerings all day long; indeed she had shrines in all the chief market places, and no one, not the humblest or most diseased, was prevented from offering there, telling his case, and receiving her answer. The other Princess, said the Rim-Shi-Ki, was scarcely of mortal birth; in her veins ran not blood but a fluid like blue air, which was the nature of blood many thousand times distilled. It was not known whether she died each day and was born afresh in the morning, or was like some flower that folds its petals at night. In her own land she was Mistress of a Magic Garden that had fallen like a cloud or a carpet into the middle of a black land which was laid with sheets of stone, the trees came up stone, and had no buds, nor were there any flowers or grass, save in this garden which was always soft as flesh. Flowers grew there with white petals; there were shadows and blue pools of water, and the Mistress lived there always in the company of birds and bees, sipping honey from lily cups, and whistling in a low sweet voice to several small animals, who were her familiars. By night she caught moon drops and wove them into fine chains of silver, which never broke, and laid them about peoples necks and led them where she chose. She had moreover dinted verses on a tablet of ivory which hung before her temple, and you must learn them to enter in. But so sharp and deep were they cut and so moon white was their brightness, that but few could say them aright, and she shot with pointed arrows all who made mistakes of sound or of grammar, so that they never dared to come again. She could weave spells for those who learnt her symbols; enchanting them with dance and song, and if she chose could shake seeds from a certain magic lily which, if planted as she told how, would bear gourds pine apples, oak trees with houses in their branches, sacred books or flocks of sheep.

"What form of worship is pleasant to these Princesses?" asked the Mandarin at length.

"Let them but see your Babies in their Baths," answered the Rim-Shi-Ki in a moment, "That is the worship they like best, or if one of you has an aged parent or a brother with a diseased leg, grant that the Princesses sit by them for a time and hear their plaints. Best of all if there is any here who visits a kinsman in the [x]Sin Sin house, permit the Princess of the Shooting Rocket to go with you."

At that time even more than now the Babies nursery was the most sacred place in the house. It was let in like a square box at the top of the stairs so that if a stork dropped a stone or a cherry tree was uprooted, the blast struck the wall and the Babe slept unharmed. And the bath which in noble houses was often formed of an ostrich egg painted with figures and in poorer houses was hollowed from a block of flawless pumice stone was always placed in the centre of the room. Nor would mothers permit bad people or ugly people or stupid people to see their children naked, for it was thought then that all qualities were of the nature of little grains, which penetrated the skin and took root and blossomed in the blood. So that the Princesses asked the most precious of privileges when they required to see a Baby in its Bath. But every Mother in the crowd at once bowed three times, and began to make off to her house, signifying with gestures of hand and head that the Princesses were immediately to follow her. Now each baby upon whom the light of their eyes fell grew up, without exception, either fair haired or dark haired, or good,

[x] Hospital.

or clever, or happy, or healthy, or rich, or in some way distinguished; at least their mothers said so; and in after life men would point in the street as some aged Mandarin with a white head passed and say "Look at the Child whom the Princess saw in his bath," which is the origin of our proverb, "Whom the Princesses loved grow old", and the reason why you should call white haired people, if you wish to please them, "The Sacred Babes".

All the most delightful things you can think of, which never happen now, happened every day while the Princesses stayed. There was chicken for dinner, and sweetmeats when you woke in the morning; once it snowed sugared almonds; another time gold pieces dropped off the laburnum trees. Only to see the Princesses pass along the streets in the morning was enough to make a grey beard chuckle in his corner, and women used to cease their baking till the cry of "The Princesses" was heard in the street, so that they might stir the crust, which is the most difficult part of baking, just as they passed. Now several sick people recovered, and the dying died, but their last words always were, "Happy am I to be the first to tell our Ghosts what has happened in Tokio". And babies had the news crooned into their ears as they were dipped for the first time, at which they always laughed, or cried, so loud that the mother knew that they were already possessed of the miraculous inspiration.

Before long it seemed good to erect a shrine to the Princesses, but the people could not agree where it was to stand; for by this time there were two different sects in Tokio, one who worshipped the Sacred Monster, another who worshipped the Lady of the Magic Garden. Each pitied the worshippers of the other, and thought them little better than Heathens. For the Sacred Monster made you laugh merely to look at her, so that you must be a happy person to begin with, which is a virtue, and she so ordered your house and family and servants and love affairs and money and garden and morals, that if you did as she bid you, you were bound to prosper in this world, and become a Mayor, and in the next still brighter crowns awaited you.

Ah, so it may be, returned the Sect of the Magic Garden, but our lady gives us something better than that. She whispers it is true, and laughs only at the time of the new Moon, when her laughter stirs ripples in the white tide all over Japan, indeed she laughs oftener than she prophecies.

But she has a charm, which once laid upon your head, as you kneel at her feet, is the most precious conceivable. By this light it appears that all the things you have toiled for, the flocks and houses and carriage horses of the rich, are become of moonshine, so that you no longer desire them, and nothing makes you laugh so much as to see the people who, as though blindfold, still pursue them. Indeed her worshippers are the merriest under the sun, for every day some great Mandarin knocks his head against a stone, or some splendid Princess thinking she has found a diamond picks up a dried chicken bone. On the other hand many trifles which we despised and hid in our cupboards, rag dolls and chop sticks and some old scrawls of parchment, become suddenly beautiful so that the very poorest, and most of her worshippers are poor, have something to take to bed with them. Our lady then is the greater of the two." -- But this the other sect denied with such fury that there might have been bloodshed, had not a wise man who was too old to believe anything, suggested that as all were agreed that the goddesses were different, they should have different shrines; one should be in the middle of the market place, like a stake in the midst of the waves, the other should be remote and high on a hilltop, where only a few wild trees grow. Thus each would have an appropriate dwelling place.

Thus it was settled, and the shrines were made and worshippers came and knelt there. And then a very odd thing happened. On the great Feast Day which was to mark the twin birthdays of the two sects, offerings were brought and laid before the shrines, fruit, vegetables, woollen underclothing, and recipes for food, before the one, broken china, rose leaf jam, and little painted books, before the other. At nightfall candles were lit, and the people withdrew, not without some emulous glances, testifying that each had prayed with more faith and sacrificed with more devotion than the other. Each left one priest to watch beside the shrine till dawn. But when morning came the good priests who had spent the night walking round and round sometimes backwards and sometimes forwards, but always with one eye on the shrine, jumped simultaneously high in the air, crying "A miracle! A miracle!" Behold all the offerings had been changed in the night and each goddess had what had been laid before the other. Who had done this? Wind or God or Man? Or Another Power which we do not name? And the next night, though the watchers were increased, the same thing happened and again before a crowd of people all open eyed as Bats, the change took place when or how none could say. Above all, what did it mean? Once more the wise old man gave his opinion.

"It is quite clear to me," he said, though he had been asleep all night, "that at a certain hour, may be two, or three, or even later, earlier perhaps, I will not be precise, that you are all of you shaken by irresistible laughter, so that your eyes are screwed into as many creases as the eyes of dormice - this is the will of the goddesses - have you laughed?"

But none had laughed.

"Very likely," he said, "you were not conscious of it; the deeper laughter is the less a man knows he is laughing; so that you may well have laughed so hard that you felt as grave as corpses - but tell me - were there any Owls abroad?"

"Not one was seen Sir."

"How should it have been seen," asked the old gentleman angrily, "the very proof that there was an owl is that no one saw it. Either my friends your eyes were shut with laughter or which is perhaps more likely, closed by the passage of an Owl's wing between you and the moon, at which moment the goddesses changed their offerings."

"Truth was never more true," said the people. "But why did they do it? Gods keep their offerings, or eat their offerings, none have been known to exchange them."

"Precisely so," said the old gentleman, "but it is quite clear that these goddesses come from a land where everything is up side down. I thought so directly I saw them. So that, if you wish to give them anything of yours, you must take something of theirs, just as when they are idle they work, when they are sad they are happy, when they die they live, and so on, and thus if you wish to worship and not to defile, the sect of the one will always worship at the shrine of the other. That my friends is the meaning of the exchange of offerings."

The worship might be going on to this day, but that the worshippers became so mixed, their rites so extravagant, their behaviour so odd, some gave all their money to hospitals and lived on the charity of their friends, others gave up their own businesses and managed those of other people, one took another's wife, and lent him his own, one jumped into a river alive and came out dead, that the shrines were closed by public order, and no worship was permitted save a silent one. The time had not come the worshippers said, or perhaps the old gentleman had been mistaken.

Now one morning all the sleepers in Tokio were woken by such a howling that they thought that their neighbours donkey had once more trod upon a snake[x], but when they ran into the

[x] A Japanese proverb.

streets all was ashen pale as though the sun had not yet risen, and nothing was to be seen. A dreadful quaking beset their bones, and they moaned and chattered like evil spirits shut out from the graves and now and then a howling rolled down the streets like cold clouds of incense. Before one such blast they fled to the hill top, and looking fearfully into the bay beneath saw a vast wave, with a curved back and silver ripples on it, rise from the floor of the sea to the summit; only it was no wave, but a monster. Out of his nostrils came two columns of steam, frizzling the air all round them, and his eyes were red caverns. Now they had just made up their minds to be devoured, when the two Princesses came down to the sea shore and bewitched the monster by making passes with certain magic wands called "Umbrellas". He turned livid, and his skin peeled off him in dry scales, and his eyes grew white like those of a stranded cod fish; a great gash opened in his back, from which a swarm of ant-like spirits came pouring, obedient to the summons of their mistresses. They gave one look at the town and at the hill, laughed and waved their arms once more; at that moment the sun burst forth like a rushing yellow globe, and the Princesses spread their tails and leapt onto the monsters back, and could be seen standing on the ridge of his nose, prodding it with pointed spears so that he gulped and took to the water again, heading out to sea. The slime of his tail lay glistening on the waves. That was the last that was ever seen of the Sacred Princesses, but if you are a good child and go to sleep, perhaps one day they will come again."

Indeed the child had been asleep these two hours—that was part of the virtue of the story, and the mother also had put the last stitch in her embroidery, and was ready to sleep too.

AFTERWORD

"MISS VIOLET DICKINSON grew to be as tall as the tallest hollyhock in the garden before she was eight." Whimsical in its simplicity, this pronouncement stages a familiar dilemma. Low-growing, sweet-scented violets represent modesty and virtue; over-tall, brilliant-hued hollyhocks signify female ambition. Virtue or ambition: what is the measure of a woman? Miss Violet Dickinson refuses the choice. Against the mandate that "if you are not to be a Maypole of Derision you must see to it that you shine forth as a Beacon of Godliness," Violet—like the real-life woman who inspired these stories—finds happiness in a "cottage of one's own" with the resonantly Shakespearean name of Burnham Wood. "This was the beginning of revolution," the narrator says of a house whose very name conjures what is seemingly impossible: a movable forest (or "Magic Garden") that vanquishes tyranny by summoning heroic courage to new ground. The narrator's words speak, simultaneously, to this moment in Virginia Woolf's artistic maturation. *The Life of Violet* is the most complete and complex of Woolf's early unpublished fictions, a daring mock-biography about a heroine who upsets, redirects, converts, and imagines anew the architectures connecting past to present. These madcap adventures envision worlds shaped by friendship among women. They also launch Woolf's challenges to Thomas Carlyle's formidable thesis that "The History of the world is but the Biography of great men."[1] *The Life of*

FIG. 3. Violet's cottage, Burnham Wood, in Welwyn, Hertfordshire. Henry W. and Albert A. Berg Collection of English and American Literature, The New York Public Library. "Burnham Wood, Welwyn—Herts," The New York Public Library Digital Collections, 1859–1939.

Violet—published here for the first time in its finished state—establishes Woolf's career-spanning conviction that to reinvent literary form is to reconceive women's lives.

The Life of Violet's feminist velocity originates not with Virginia Woolf's literary aspirations but with Violet Dickinson herself. Nigel Nicolson's preface to volume 1 of *The Letters of Virginia Woolf* introduces Violet in terms that have, regrettably, come to define her. This friend with whom Virginia shared seemingly every thought during her twenties, Nicolson tells us, was "gawky, even graceless, but everybody who knew her in the literary and fashionable world which she frequented, adored her. . . . More than half the letters in this volume were written to her, and but for them she might be quite forgotten" (xviii). Channeling Nicolson's sentiments, scholars tend to regard Violet as a minor character in the story of Woolf's career, an early intimate who would be supplanted by Vita Sackville-West (1892–1962) and Ethel Smyth (1858–1944).[2] But the publication of *The Life of Violet* occasions a welcome reframing of its title character's remarkable eighty-three years. As Woolf knew, and took pains to underscore in the interconnected stories collected here, "the life of Miss Violet Dickinson is one of the most singular as well as the most prolific and least notorious that was lived in our age."

Mary Violet Dickinson burst into the world on April 24, 1865, weighing almost ten pounds and, according to her mother's diary, "very fat and happy."[3] She was the only daughter and the third of four children born to Emily Dulcibella Eden (1833–93) and Edmund Henry Dickinson (1821–97). On her father's side, she descended from a Somerset family made wealthy by the transatlantic slave trade and sugar plantations in Jamaica; on her mother's, a distinguished baronetcy whose members were bishops, parliamentarians, and powerful administrators of Britain's overseas domains.[4] Violet's unusual proportions distinguished her from infancy onward and, in part, emboldened her resistance to the conventions of nineteenth-century aristocratic girlhood. A posthumous biographical sketch of Violet authored by one of her Dickinson relatives offers the droll suggestion that "being planted on clay soil at Berkley in Somersetshire accounted for her abnormal development in height" (DD/DN/5/6/3 [120]) and reports that this ninth-generation Dickinson daughter hated dolls and casual conversation. Violet grew into an adolescent who stymied the traditional rites of passage for young ladies: "Her education was undertaken by a succession of 8 old or inexperienced young governesses producing feeble results . . . [H]er scattered mind gained strange information and experience from her friends and books, for three months spent in London every spring for needed polish in the way of classes and dancing" (DD/DN/5/6/3 [122]). If Violet's full height of six feet two eventually rendered her unmarriageable (as Woolf quipped in 1937, "Am I right in saying that to be 6 ft tall in the Age of Q. Victoria was equivalent to having an illegitimate child?"),[5] her enjoyment of "strange information and experience" nevertheless fostered a vibrant adult life. Friendship itself became her career.

Violet's social ties flourished within and without the aristocratic and political circles of her birth. At thirty-four, she served as mayoress of Bath during her brother Robert Dickinson's term as mayor from 1899 to 1900, accompanying him for public appearances wearing an extravagant, custom-made, jeweled brooch still displayed in the Bath Guildhall.[6] She was a very close friend of the writer Kate Greenaway, a prolific author and illustrator of Victorian children's literature whose biography highlighted Violet's influence. ("It strikes me that you are really something of a celebrity" [*L1*, 205], Woolf would write to Violet on reading *The Life of Kate Greenaway* in 1905.[7]) Violet was also an intimate of the family of John Thynne, 4th Marquess of Bath, and grew especially close to his daughters, Beatrice and Katherine Thynne, spending nearly every Christmas at Longleat House in Wiltshire and bequeathing many of her papers to the family's estate upon her death in 1948. From 1902 on, Violet welcomed guests to Burnham Wood, the cottage she built in Welwyn, Hertfordshire, and shared with her brother Oswald, with whom she also shared a London home in Manchester Street. Among the friends who frequented these residences was the writer and suffragist Lady Eleanor ("Nelly") Cecil and her husband, the future Nobel laureate Lord Robert Cecil, whom Violet accompanied on a dazzling round-the-world cruise in 1905. We will return to this voyage (and the elaborate album

Violet created to commemorate it) for its foundational role in *The Life of Violet*'s third chapter, "A Story to Make You Sleep."

Violet was as generous a caregiver as she was a hostess. It is well known that Virginia Woolf convalesced at Burnham Wood following a breakdown in the spring of 1904 and that Violet nursed her back to health.[8] It is less well known that Violet's support extended beyond the sickroom and into literary domains: she wrote a pseudonymous eighteen-page "tract" titled *These Thoughts Were Written By Anthony Harte* and sent it to Virginia, who was in London chafing under the strict eye of the Stephen family physician, Dr. George Savage. Violet's booklet, handsewn and bound between plain red covers, its individual sections separated by the small printer's motif of a violet, adopts a convincingly high-flown seventeenth-century idiom to address "them upon whom the burden of sicknesse has fallen" and urges those so afflicted to "eschew dwelling upon their pain, weariness and miserie."[9] Woolf was impressed with Violet's skilled creation of a fictional voice—"Anthony Harte is her own writing!" she exclaims in her diary—and seized on one particular metaphor that expressed something of Violet Dickinson's own philosophy of human relations: "As an atom of dust doth cause a loud sneeze in the nostril, so at times doth a tiny kindnesse bring forth a glow of happinesse in the lonelie heart."[10] "I like the great sneeze!" Woolf wrote to Violet, praising the tract's persuasive directives about hope and health and promising that "my weary nights which aren't really weary, will be sweetened and made profitable" (*L1*, 175).[11]

Indeed, Violet "sweetened and made profitable" an assortment of different and differently troubled lives over the years, forming connections that her familial biographer describes as mutually beneficial: "In middle age . . . [r]ich and poor, Saints and Sinners could be found among her friends; unfailing in prosperity and in affliction they rallied to her aid" (DD/DN/5/6/3 [123]). From 1917 to 1920, Violet made weekly visits to the Farmfield Reformatory for Inebriate Women, where inmates would tell her about lives marked by addiction, crime, suicide attempts, and other traumas. Violet danced and sang with these women; she played games and ran races; one Christmas, she watched them put on a dramatic play about a courtroom trial. She gave encouraging weekly addresses to the reformatory's nurses and staff, likening them, in her final speech in 1920, to English water lilies enriched rather than harmed by the mud that surrounds them.[12] After Farmfield closed, Violet's cheery disposition brightened patients' days in the Policeman's Hospital; she also made "visits to the London Hospital for many years" (DD/DN/5/6/3 [123]). Woolf may have composed *The Life of Violet* a decade prior to her friend's postwar doings, but she correctly intuited how Violet's "half thoughts born in the Somersetshire school room, growing by fits and London drawing rooms, hospitals and streets fixed on other people and started eddies in their blood, which drove them to all kinds of unforeseen experiences."

A minor anecdote from Violet's later years illustrates the still-visible effects of a generosity that extended beyond England's shores. In 1943, Violet learned that the Orientalist scholar, collector, and captain George Humphreys-Davies was building a collection of Asian arts for the Auckland Museum in New Zealand. The city of Auckland had been named for Violet's great-uncle and governor-general of India, George Eden, 1st Earl of Auckland, and Violet, excited about adding a new dimension to this familial connection, initiated a correspondence with Humphreys-Davies. To enrich the museum's holdings of Asian fine and decorative arts, she donated Chinese, Japanese, Persian, and Indian art objects—including a beautiful comb once belonging to the powerful Chinese dowager empress Cixi (1835–1908)—that she had inherited, collected on her travels, or acquired as gifts over her lifetime.[13] Like the mayoress's brooch displayed in the Bath Guildhall, objects from Violet's bequest can be seen in the Auckland Museum today, each one embodying its own artisanal genealogy and the interconnected histories of trade routes, imperial authority, and diplomatic gift exchange.

We know these facts about Violet Dickinson's life because—as we have already seen with *These Thoughts Were Written By Anthony Harte*—she herself was a writer. Violet's assorted and still-unpublished autobiographical writings include an elegant tribute to Burnham Wood and several essays, vignettes, and stories (among them her "Memoir of the Stephen Family," the work I was seeking when I discovered *The Life of Violet*).[14] A dedicated documentarian of family history, Violet wrote and illustrated a lively preface for an edition of Jonathan Dickinson's *God's Protecting Providence* (1699), her paternal Quaker ancestor's widely read account of shipwreck and captivity on the Florida coast while sailing from Jamaica to Philadelphia.[15] Her contributions fill the pages of the *Manuscript History of the Dickinson Family*, a multiauthored record of ten generations over three centuries. She edited and compiled ten volumes of the eighteenth- and nineteenth-century history of her maternal Eden family, a massive undertaking that involved transcribing letters, diaries, and autobiographies as well as collecting original artwork.[16] This latter project extended the work Violet had done to produce *Miss Eden's Letters* (1919), an edited collection of correspondence by her great-aunt Emily Eden (1797–1869), a highly regarded painter, travel writer, and novelist.[17] Published by Macmillan, praised by Lytton Strachey, and reviewed generously in the *Times Literary Supplement* by Woolf, *Miss Eden's Letters* is a vital contribution to the history of women's arts and letters in England, exemplifying Woolf's claim a decade later in *A Room of One's Own* that "we think back through our mothers if we are women" (75).[18] Indeed, an 1834 letter by Emily Eden uncannily anticipates Woolf's thesis in *A Room of One's Own* that "a woman must have money and a room of her own if she is to write fiction" (4): "I wish I could write like Mrs. Hannah More," Violet's great-aunt opined, applauding her eighteenth-century playwright-philanthropist predecessor, "and have money enough to build myself a Barley Wood, and resolution to go and live there" (*Miss Eden's Letters*, 243).

Violet's dedication to preserving genealogical and biographical records remained robust until the end of her life. In 1936, she returned hundreds of Woolf's letters, a gesture that startled Woolf and that scholars have read as Violet's plea to rekindle a friendship that had diminished two decades earlier.[19] But Woolf was only one among many correspondents whose letters Violet returned. After making typed copies of letters she had received over five decades from more than 140 friends and acquaintances—including Lady Margot Asquith, George Bernard Shaw, Constance Lytton, and Janet Case—Violet returned the originals to their senders or their families. Her meticulously labeled copies, neatly bound in two large volumes and interspersed with photographs and drawings of their authors, reveal multiple aspects of a life that extended well beyond the social boundaries of Somerset aristocracy. Little wonder, then, that Woolf exhorted her friend to "scribble me your memoirs. . . . How you could describe the Duckworths, the Stephens, let alone the Thynnes, and the ancient nobility of England!" (*L1*, 158).

I do not wish to suggest that Violet was a professional archivist or writer, or to identify her with a radicalism that she never embraced. (She did not disguise her disapproval, for instance, when Leslie Stephen's daughters left South Kensington to settle in Bloomsbury, and she never turned her back on the aristocratic world of her birth.[20]) But like her more famous friend, Violet devoted herself to illuminating the life stories of ordinary and extraordinary women. Indeed, a mutual curiosity about those stories was integral to her friendship with Virginia from the outset, and, in my view, commands greater significance for feminist literary history than the compassionate nurturing that dominates accounts of Violet and Woolf's relationship.[21]

Consider Woolf's first detailed description of Violet, a 1902 diary entry made when Violet joined the Stephen family during a holiday in the New Forest. Playfully dubbing her friend "Aunt Maria," twenty-year-old Woolf styles Violet as a force disruptive to social and narrative expectations about women:

> Beatrice [Thynne] had left us for two or three days when Aunt Maria came. And lest anyone should supply the figure of an ancient maiden lady, with white curls & a parrot to fit this name, I think it most honest to state at once that Aunt Maria is 37 years of age—Six feet two in height & of an appearance that is all that Aunt Marias ought not to be—Whence then the name? That, as a popular writer says, is another story, to which we may come in the course of time.[22]

These lines burst with early signs of *The Life of Violet*'s three chapters: the unconventional Violet realigns the coordinates of late Victorian femininity and merits "another story" precisely because she is "all that Aunt Marias ought not to be." When Violet's carriage crosses paths with a New Forest stag hunt, Woolf revels in the contrast between the unrestrained masculine physicality of the "flight of panting riders, & mad splashed horses" and the genteel appurtenances of the female traveler:

> It was the most comical sight—the rusty old fly—the conventional ark shaped box—the London-looking lady, with her little handbags & brown paper parcels—suddenly caught up in

> the middle of a hunting scene which might have ridden straight out of a Graphic Christmas number. But Aunt Maria appreciated the situation only her one wish was to get out & follow the hounds. When she had paid her flyman, & told him to take her box to the house, she gathered up her skirts, & ran as fast as her long legs would carry her. (SxMs-18-2-A-26.74–75)

If the true-to-form hunt seems to have leaped from the pages of the popular Victorian periodical *The Graphic*, Violet herself breaks the mold, running, skirts lifted, away from the house and toward the hounds. It is a small but telling instance of why Woolf esteemed a friend who was "always talking & laughing & entering into whatever was going on with a most youthful zeal" (SxMs-18-2-A-26.77), and why she scorned as "superficial indeed" anyone who dismissed Violet as "one of those cleverish adaptable ladies of middle age who are welcome everywhere & not indispensable anywhere" (SxMs-18-2-A-26.78). Invisible and hypervisible, everywhere and nowhere: this paradoxical state of being, Woolf knew, was assumed to be the inevitable destiny of those deemed "odd women," a painfully apt term for hollyhock-tall Violet. *The Life of Violet* remakes the narrative logic of biography to upend such assumptions. Bending time and space to reveal her friend's gifts, Woolf realizes through literature freedoms greater than those afforded to Violet by history.

Drafted in 1907 and revised in 1908, *The Life of Violet* reflects the peak of a creative ferment that had accelerated after the death of Woolf's father, Leslie Stephen, in 1904. Few episodes in Woolf's life have been as exhaustively studied as her move from South Kensington to Bloomsbury, and I will not rehearse her storied escape from late-Victorian mores here except to touch briefly on those elements that informed *The Life of Violet*. The domestic milieux Woolf created with her siblings—first at

46 Gordon Square, and then, following her brother Thoby's death from typhoid in 1906 and her sister Vanessa's 1907 marriage to Clive Bell, with her younger brother Adrian at 29 Fitzroy Square—thrummed with social and artistic potential. Her newfound social circles, which had not yet cohered into what we refer to as "the Bloomsbury Group," offered sparkling intellectual energy in gatherings such as Thoby's "Thursday Evenings," Vanessa's Friday Club, and the Play Reading Society she and Adrian hosted at Fitzroy Square. Woolf's authorial aspirations acquired fresh dimensions as she traveled with family and friends (including Violet) to Spain, Portugal, France, Italy, Greece, and Turkey. Each international journey, like the numerous trips she took within England, played an enduring role in her sense of literary possibility, shining through *The Life of Violet*, and, later, her full-length novels. Woolf expanded her linguistic repertoire, adding Spanish, Italian, and German to an already advanced knowledge of Latin and Greek, and she worked as a teacher at Morley College in London, teaching English composition and literature to working-class students. Above all, she read, feeding passions captured eloquently in a diary entry written the year before her father's death:

> [T]he books are the things that I enjoy—on the whole—most. I feel sometimes for hours together as though the physical stuff of my brain were expanding, larger & larger, throbbing quicker & quicker with new blood --& there is no more delicious sensation than this. I read some history: it is suddenly all alive, branching forwards & backwards & connected with every kind of thing that seemed entirely remote before. I seem to feel Napoleons influence on our quiet evening in the garden for instance—I think I see for a moment how our minds are all threaded together—how

> any live mind today is of the very same stuff as Plato's & Euripides. It is only a continuation & development of the same thing. It is this common mind that binds the whole world together; & all the world is mind. (*PA*, 179)

It was Violet Dickinson who enabled Woolf to channel this vibrant sense of interconnectedness into a paying profession.

Violet read many of Virginia's writings and recognized the breadth of her talents.[23] In 1904, she introduced Virginia to Kathleen Lyttelton, editor of the Women's Supplement for *The Guardian* (a clerical paper unrelated to today's newspaper of the same name), who invited Virginia to contribute to the paper. The more than sixty pieces Woolf published between 1904 and 1907 in *The Guardian* and other newspapers and periodicals supply evidence of erudition as well as genius.[24] In essays, reviews, and obituaries, Woolf reveals her command of the British literary canon across multiple genres (e.g., Shakespeare, Sydney, Wordsworth, Dickens, the Carlyles); she illuminates the merits of new novels from a transatlantic canon-in-the-making (by, e.g., Henry James, Edith Wharton, Winston Churchill, William Dean Howells); and she mixes memoir and cultural commentary in chronicles of her own travels through Spain and England. Her reverence for the essay as an art form emerges in pieces about subjects ranging from the Brontë parsonage and street musicians to women memoirists.

It was also at this time that Woolf made her first adult forays into writing fiction. (Her juvenilia is preserved in the *Hyde Park Gate News,* the Stephen children's newspaper that ended in 1895 when Julia Stephen died.) Her early stories are transparently autobiographical sketches about young ladies trapped by the imperative to marry. Those that survive are unevenly paced and tentative, and in this regard, very unlike her paid writing for newspapers and periodicals. But her mock-biography of Violet Dickinson was a breakthrough. It is the longest and only multichapter fictional work from this period, and its investigation of how to narrate a woman's life took Woolf into new literary terrain. Indisputably, *The Life of Violet* lacks the technical sophistication that Woolf would bring a decade later to "The Mark on the Wall" or "Kew Gardens"; nor can it keep company with Woolf's shimmering treatment of consciousness, memory, and time in *Mrs. Dalloway* or *To the Lighthouse*. What makes *The Life of Violet* significant in Woolf's writerly evolution is its surefooted, self-conscious critique of *where* the architecture of fiction demands renovation.

Woolf's mouthpiece for this critique is *The Life of Violet*'s narrator—unnamed, male, lower- or working-class, living "in a garret with one dirty charwoman who brings me Lloyds Weekly and a bunch of kippered herrings tied by the tails"—who, to my ear, is one of the most engaging and underappreciated voices she created. This narrator alternately subverts and agonizes over the problems of genre that Woolf would solve in the 1920s and 1930s. Beset with anxieties about rules, limits, and the proprieties of class, he promises that "we shall move in good society" as we follow Violet's antics. He assures us that he is "a sincere historian" and that "this Biography is no novel but a sober chronicle." Leaving out a great many things, *The Life of Violet*'s narrator insists on his trustworthiness ("we are writing no novel but the essence of truth") as he cites limitations on his time and withholds details that it would be "neither polite nor possible" to supply. The source of his originality is his relationship to the very language that is his medium. Introducing himself as a man forced to speak in an adopted language, the narrator claims that he would impart more information to us "if I had the freedom of my mother tongue, as I have it not, for a reason to be told in the appendix." However, both his actual mother tongue and the cause for its suppression remain mysterious, because (a brilliant comic touch!) the putative appendix is "missing." After delivering the first two stories in what we infer is borrowed or secondary English, the narrator performs a ventriloquist feat in "A Story to Make You Sleep." Foregrounding the artistic dangers of crossing between languages, he speaks in the voice of a Japanese mother addressing her child. "Mine of course is but the English version," he apologizes for his rendition of "a story fast becoming a myth," acknowledging that "all the delicate rose pinks and silvers are rubbed off it, as a schoolboy's thumb will obliterate the wing of a Peach Blossom Moth." Here are transformations, approximations, rebirths: Japanese prose translated into (non-native) English, a story elevated from the domestic to the mythic, a man's voice vanishing into the voice of a woman thinking back through her mother ("I can but tell you what my mother told me and her mother told her"). What are a story's—and before that, a person's—points of origin? How little we know "man-woman-or Violet kind," the narrator observes, his plurilingual voice enacting the classic Woolfian principle that literature, like selfhood, is immanently protean.

To be sure, it is tempting to read *The Life of Violet* primarily as a cloud-light roman à clef. Woolf troubles herself very little to disguise the titled, wealthy friends who inspired her characters: Lady Bath and two of her daughters, Lady Beatrice Thynne and Lady Katherine Thynne Cromer; Lady Eleanor (Nelly) Cecil; Mrs. Kitty Lushington Maxse; Mrs. Ella Sieveking Crum. These women had entered Virginia's life while she was still living at 22 Hyde Park Gate and caring for her widowed father. She met them largely through her association with Violet Dickinson and moved cautiously in their world; they offered Virginia, the daughter of an educated professional who was neither a

FIG. 4. Frances Isabella Catherine Vesey, Lady Bath, 1870s. Photographed by Alexander Bassano. Albumen. The Royal Photographic Society Collection at the V&A, acquired with the generous assistance of the National Lottery Heritage Fund and Art Fund.

landowner nor a titled member of the gentry, what Sonya Rudikoff calls "aristocracy for beginners."[25] Most of these women did not have children—Beatrice Thynne, like Violet, never married—and they were, as Hermione Lee observes, "all unusual." Fascinated by her new friends' ease and majesty, Virginia wrote about them in language that anticipates *The Life of Violet*. A 1903 tableau titled "An Afternoon with the Pagans" describes Katie Thynne as "a divine Giantess" with "superb limbs" who pulls a pump handle in her garden until her sister Beatrice shrieks comically, "Well Katie—you have had a brilliant idea . . . its the drains" (*PA*, 185). A letter written in 1907 characterizes Violet, Lady Nelly, and Kitty Maxse as "beings moving in a higher world, with voices like the ripple of Arcadian streams" (*L1*, 297), and another, written after a fallow social period, confesses, "I am pining for my garden of beautiful women" (*L1*, 311).

Nevertheless, Woolf came to associate these women with a conventionality that tinted her affection with skepticism. They represented for her the insularity of the peerage and of a femininity predicated upon artifice; moreover, she had long disdained any social architecture designed to foster marriages between desirable parties.[26] (As she announced in an oft-quoted letter to her cousin Emma Vaughan, "I am going to found a colony where there shall be no marrying—unless you happen to fall in love with a symphony of Beethoven—no human element at all, except what comes through Art—nothing but ideal peace and endless meditation" [*L1*, 41–42].)[27] *The Life of Violet* makes hay of aristocratic lives built around inheritance and continuity, its drawing-room and country-house antics earning Woolf a place in the Wilde-Waugh-Wodehouse canon. But parody and caricature, however amusing, reveal themselves to be insufficiently literary for Woolf's aims. Each chapter in *The Life of Violet* diverts attention *away* from correspondences

FIG. 5. Kitty Maxse, 1922. Sepia photograph by W&D Downey, London. Mary Evans Picture Library.

FIG. 6. Lady Beatrice Thynne, 1923. Photographed by Alexander Bassano. Half-plate glass negative. © National Portrait Gallery, London.

Lady Robert Cecil
as Valentine Visconti (XV Century)

FIG. 7. Eleanor (née Lambton), Viscountess Cecil of Chelwood, as Valentina Visconti (XV Century), 1897. Alfred Ellis Walker & Boutall. Photogravure. © National Portrait Gallery, London.

between characters and their real-life counterparts, suggesting that laughter itself transforms narrative more powerfully than the exaggerated gestures of caricature. To put this differently: Woolf views laughter not only as a desired effect of her stories but as each plot line's climactic force.

Woolf's 1905 essay "The Value of Laughter" furnishes a language for understanding how *The Life of Violet* distances itself from parody and incorporates what Woolf calls "the comic spirit" into each chapter. This spirit, Woolf argues, "concerns itself with oddities and eccentricities and deviation from the recognised pattern"; it compels us to laugh and "preserves our sense of proportion."[28] Thus, it is not only narrative commentary that strips away pretense but the bodily phenomenon of the characters' own laughter. In "Friendships Gallery," unexpected laughter twice changes the course of young Violet Dickinson's fortunes, first when she and the Peer laugh at her gold cross during the ball, quashing any potential romantic entanglement, and next when her visage and jokes make Lady . . . . laugh: "[H]er Ladyship's sense of humour was tickled, and she was grateful to any one who made her laugh; 'I like sneezing and I like laughing,' she used to say, 'but it must be natural.'" In "The Magic Garden," Violet embarks on building her cottage after piercing the proprieties of Hatfield House with anecdotes about the revolutionary figure of their gardener ("obeying some native instinct that was certainly not polite, gave such a picture drawn in coloured detail of the Cookson family, that no one could help laughing; no one had been heard to laugh so loud for twenty or thirty or forty years"). And laughter suffuses "A Story to Make You Sleep," starting with the otherworldly pair of goddess-giantess-princess-monsters who appear in Japan, one who "made you laugh merely to look at her" and the other who "laughs oftener than she prophecies":

> Whether they had tails nobody could say; they had great brown hoofs, and they made a noise as they walked, not like our speech, but like the noise that clappers made shaken by boys in the rice fields to scare crows, and now and then there was a scale of bells, beginning high and running all the way down, as an opossum with an ivory tail comes down stairs. They had large eyes, like eggs, filled with fire to the brim, great teeth, much fur like hair, which had built a kind of birds nest on the top of their heads, where strange fruits grew and glossy leaves. They did not walk as we do, one foot before the other, but gave long springs, now this side and now that, like a puma cat.

These are "oddities and eccentricities and deviation from the recognised pattern" indeed—and on confronting the spectacle of these two creatures, "instead of feeling a cold shudder in the marrow bones and exorcising it with prayers our ancestors could do nothing but laugh." Undoing and remaking women's bodies and language, Woolf fuses elements of the animal, the human, the cosmic, and the divine in hybrid creatures untethered by the rules restraining her readers. And if the chimerical female figures in "A Story to Make You Sleep" look back to ancient mythologies, their extraordinary aspect also portends the laughter-centered, multigenre twentieth-century experiments of Leonora Carrington, Edward Gorey, and Salman Rushdie.

The Life of Violet marks a literary turning point, weaving together the passions and commitments we associate with Woolf's later works. Its mock-heroic mode, as Karin Westman observes, is "the complex root-system from which *Orlando* [1928] grows." Its casual statement "the very proof that there was an owl is that no one saw it" alludes to debates about reality and perception that play a central role in *To the Lighthouse*.[29] It also offers a glimpse of the egalitarian societies Woolf would promote in *A Room of One's Own* (1929) and *Three Guineas* (1938); and we can recognize in Violet the first of the "daughters of educated men" who might have claimed membership in *Three Guineas*'s "Society of Outsiders," an imaginary collective of Englishwomen committed to attaining "justice and equality and liberty for all men and women."[30] The governess-educated aristocratic daughter—a stock Victorian trope—becomes a renegade who renders the canon of male-authored English literature inseparable from the biographies of ordinary women:

> Shakespeares pages were stamped with the affairs of the heart of Mademoiselle Bourget; Keats sang of German life in a flat on the third story; Wordsworth taught her how a plain Somersetshire girl, the daughter of an Attorney can earn her living, hem her underclothing, and keep her father's drunkenness from the knowledge of the neighbours. If you ask her to quote the Ode to Duty, at this day, which she thinks the finest modern poem, and she keeps it by her bedside, she will at once tell you the story of Miss Janet Sitwell.

And the ongoing challenges of *The Life of Violet*'s narrator-biographer will be instantly familiar to readers of Woolf's literary and biographical works, as when the narrator despairs of conveying Violet's true character: "Often she has whisked behind a paragraph and it was only when I had done it and set it proudly in its place in the pile raised to her honour that I discovered that she was behind and not in front, that I had made a screen and no pane of glass." Such metatextual moments presage the dilemmas of Woolf's artist-protagonists (the painter Lily Briscoe in *To the Lighthouse*; the pageant director Miss LaTrobe in *Between the Acts* [1941]) as well as the theories of life writing Woolf expresses magnificently in her 1939 essay, "The Art of

Biography," and tests in her own memoir, *A Sketch of the Past* (1939–41).

But it is also crucial to recognize that *The Life of Violet* is a singularity, a three-part fictional biography with an antiplot unlike anything its author wrote subsequently. *The Life of Violet* shows us a Woolf who *might have been*—a fabulist unmaking patriarchy's cultural inheritances through enchanting, surreal impossibilities rather than philosophy or history. Woolf does not work in the idiom she created for *The Life of Violet* after 1908. Later biographical inventions may play with elements of the fantastic (sex change and time travel in *Orlando*), the fanciful (the dog's-eye view of human relations in *Flush*), or the farcical (an artistic coterie's exaggerated eccentricities in her little-known comic play *Freshwater*), but Woolf's evolving granite-and-rainbow vision of reality turns increasingly, inescapably historical. *The Life of Violet* stands apart from its successors by rendering the canons of history (and their attendant literary forms) illegible as well as irrelevant. "Friendships Gallery" flings away the marriage plot and English history alike—in fact, the story's sole proposal occurs when the Peer proposes to bury Violet's cross during the ball!—and ends with the narrator's realization that human character comes into being through forces beyond language: "no prose, as I begin to discover, can tell you how Irish mists break over Lancashire rods of steel in the brain of their descendant." "The Magic Garden" draws to a close with the narrator's refusal to specify Burnham Wood's value in historical terms ("It would take me at least two more chapters to write out the significance of the place in the life of the time"). Finally, "A Story to Make You Sleep," cast in mythic time, banishes history altogether, refusing to refract human experience through the divisions of clock and calendar.

"A Story to Make You Sleep" has its roots in the round-the-world voyage Violet took in 1905 with Lady Nelly and her husband, the future League of Nations architect and Nobel Peace Prize laureate, Lord Robert Cecil. It was a moment that saw a crescendo in British and US diplomatic outreach to East Asia and, in fact, Violet's journey coincided with the Asian tour of a US delegation led by President Theodore Roosevelt's secretary of state, William Howard Taft.[31] Violet memorialized the five-month trip in an enormous album—a fabulous archival object in itself—whose pages contain dozens of neatly captioned photographs interspersed with newspaper clippings, handwritten itineraries, Lady Nelly's colored pencil sketches, and other ephemera.[32] To the cinema-trained twenty-first-century eye, Violet's album is the stuff of period drama, the glamorous aura of steamship travel captured in photographs of English ladies in long white gowns and large beribboned hats, accompanied on deck by cigar-smoking English gentlemen whose beautiful cravats set off their tailored suits. And the eight-country trip itself held plenty of glamour, as Violet had "companions beyond praise" (DD/DN/5/6/3 [123]), in the words of her anonymous Somerset biographer, from the moment she sailed from Liverpool to Quebec on the RMS *Victorian,* one of the new turbine-powered ocean liners ushering in an age of luxury cruises.

Violet and the Cecils were hosted by royalty, heads of state, and other luminaries at each destination. They toured Quebec and Montreal, meeting the Canadian prime minister, Sir Wilfrid Laurier and Lady Laurier, and then, "with 22 bits of luggage,"[33] rode the trans-Canadian Pacific Railway to Vancouver, stopping in Banff where they were received by the superintendent of National Parks. From Vancouver, they sailed on the RMS *Empress of China* to Yokohama. A monthlong stay in Japan took them to Tokyo, where they dined with Emperor Mutsuhito, and then to Nikko, Nagoya, Kamakura, Kyoto, Kobe, and Nagasaki; they saw Buddhist and Shinto temples, horse races, wrestling matches, and a newly built hospital. The SS *Mongolia* (coincidentally, the sister ship of the *Manchuria*, which was transporting Taft's US delegation) then bore them to Shanghai, Hong Kong, Singapore, Penang, and Colombo. Sailing on the SS *Bremen* to end their trip in Cairo, Violet, Nelly, and Lord Robert enjoyed luxurious city tours and excursions to the Pyramids and the Sphinx as guests of the consul general of Egypt, Lord Cromer and Lady Cromer (formerly Katie Thynne). Lord Curzon, recently viceroy of India, was a fellow passenger on the return journey to England in December.[34]

The entire trip fired Woolf's imagination. She marveled at the "6 separate lists of addresses, which are all ingeniously varied" (*L1*, 209) where she was to write to her friends, and mused, before posting a letter, "I feel that these words ought to be more durable than brass to travel all the way—where? Singapore, or Yokohama." Japan, more than any other destination on the voyage, fascinated her. In letters to Nelly, Woolf boasts of her own knowledge about Japan: "By the way, I read that the Japanese bathe always three times a day: Sometimes more often," she writes just before the voyage, and declares, two months later, "I am an authority upon Japan now; I daresay I shall be given the Japanese books to do for the Times" (*L1*, 211). She offers Nelly this lofty pronouncement: "The one quality lacking in Japan is what the Greeks (and the Cockneys) call Pathos. A bare tree visible in the Light of Human Suffering means more than all the Pagodas in Tokio" (*L1*, 212). In contrast, letters to Violet trade in comedy. "Not having a map here," Woolf writes from Cornwall, "you have now sailed entirely out of my ken. My mental geography ends at America. 'Where is Yokohama?' says Nessa!" (*L1*, 205). She wonders whether "all the steerage wives

FIG. 8. Katherine Georgiana Louisa Thynne, Countess of Cromer. Photographed by H. Walter Barnett, 1901–1903. Whole-plate glass negative. © National Portrait Gallery, London.

bore their babies under your guidance," and, at the same time, teases Violet about the exalted company she keeps in Japan: "Thoby says you have all been received by the Mikado. Take care that you dont get into Punch as an international joker. I can imagine you sprawling half across a cartoon" (*L1*, 209).[35]

The contrasting tones of Woolf's 1905 letters to Violet and Nelly manifest themselves in *The Life of Violet*'s mixture of aesthetic Japonisme (a sophisticated visual language with a sweeping presence in late nineteenth-century European fine and decorative arts) and superficial japonaiserie (condescending imperial Western assumptions about Japan and an "Orient" more broadly).[36] When Woolf set out to compose *The Life of Violet*, she was conversant with Japanese-influenced forms of fin de siècle arts through the scholars, practitioners, and purveyors of Japonisme—for example, Dante Gabriel Rossetti, James Whistler, Laurence Binyon, William Morris, and Arthur Lasenby Liberty—who were part of her domestic and intellectual worlds.[37] (A teasing letter to Lady Nelly in 1901 flirts with the prospect of a literary Japonisme: "When you die," Woolf wrote to her friend, "I shall tell the truth about you. It would be a very interesting article—something like a Japanese watercolour, with an angular ivory face" [*L1*, 390].) Japonisme's visual idioms pervade *The Life of Violet* (women in the garden at Grove End Road, for example, "shook cherry blossoms from a benignant tree upon the face of a child, who crowed thereupon and clapped his hands, as at some familiar rain of crimson butterflies"), as do the perspectival possibilities of ukiyo-e, or the "floating world" of Japanese woodblocks that captured the transitory quality of the everyday, as in the narrator's depiction of the Hatfield House grounds:

> I repeat, it was summer morning, and a perfectly even sheet of air shifted up and down and smoothed the landscape like

> some subtle painters medium. Trees and little hills and far church spires all were blunted of their sharp angles, rounded and suffused, and at the same time made of solid body. [. . .] There never was a deeper or more tranquil scene, as though the colour had been steaming upwards through solid miles before it reached the earth's surface and glowed there, and as though not one yelp or discord was contained in the whole seas of air which swam continually across the sky so fine was their texture.[38]

But *The Life of Violet*'s nuanced Japonisme collides with its author's racial presumptuousness. Twenty-first-century readers need hardly be told that the nonsensical inventions of Woolf's "Tokio" in "A Story to Make You Sleep"—unlike the well-informed parodic elements of the two stories set in England—emanate from unapologetically limited cultural knowledge. Like Nanki-Poo and Yum-Yum in Gilbert and Sullivan's 1885 comic operetta *The Mikado*, Japanese names and titles in "A Story to Make You Sleep" take the form of repetitive or hyphenated monosyllables ("chin-chin"; "Rick-Shi"; "Rim-Shi-Ki") meant to sound exotic, and for which Woolf provides footnoted "translations," but that correspond to no actual meaning. The story's elaborate settings and faux-Japanese sayings and customs, similarly, echo the error-filled pretentions of Puccini's 1904 opera *Madama Butterfly*.

Without apologizing for Woolf's Orientalism, we can, simultaneously, illuminate the new social order it buttresses in "A Story to Make You Sleep." If Violet Dickinson's experience of Japan in 1905 reflected the grandeur of Britain's presence on the world stage, Woolf remakes the trip by stripping it of all historical specificity. The story dispenses almost entirely with fathers, privileging the experiences of mothers and children, and Woolf replaces the British imperial-aristocratic hierarchies of her friends' Japanese sojourn with the generative possibilities embodied by the two goddesses. The Sacred Monster's "powers were as marvellous as her height, she could heal cripples, make small children appear out of bags, marriages were made by her, she could tame wild beasts, and make surly bears dance"; while the Lady of the Magic Garden "could shake seeds from a certain magic lily," which would "bear gourds, pine apples, oak trees with houses in their branches, sacred books or flocks of sheep." When the inhabitants of Tokio erect shrines for these creatures, Woolf paints a portrait of a two-deity utopia so advanced and radically egalitarian that not even the world of the story can sustain it:

> The worship might be going on to this day, but that the worshippers became so mixed, their rites so extravagant, their behaviour so odd, some gave all their money to hospitals and lived on the charity of their friends, others gave up their own businesses and managed those of other people, one took another's wife, and lent him his own, one jumped into a river alive and came out dead, that the shrines were closed by public order, and no worship was permitted save a silent one. The time had not come the worshippers said.

"The time had not come": as though to emphasize that a society of unceasing free exchange, however desirable, eludes the grasp of mortals, Woolf reminds us that this is a bedtime story for a child who "had been asleep these two hours—that was part of the virtue of the story." The Sacred Princesses depart Tokio on the back of a sea monster, their destinies forever unknown to characters and readers alike, and the story itself melts into the dream-consciousness of a child who may never recollect hearing it. Resemblances between "A Story to Make You Sleep" and Violet and Nelly's travels cease to matter. Moreover, it is a feminist triumph to concoct a fairy-tale ending untouched by the questions of virtue and ambition that had troubled young Violet in "Friendships Gallery."

Woolf first mentioned the idea for *The Life of Violet* in the spring of 1907: "I am going to write a book upon the Aesthetic Sense in Violet and Nelly" (*L1*, 295), she wrote to Violet. In August, Vanessa expressed her eagerness to read this new work: ("Have you finished your Life of Violet yet? If so do send it to me, and any other works I haven't seen").[39] Virginia mailed a draft to Violet in early August, intent on keeping her creation private: "Here is this work, very hastily polished off this morning . . . however you and Nelly are to be the only readers" (*L1*, 303). She repeated the request for privacy to Nelly: "If you keep the Life, or Myth," she wrote to her friend, "dont quote it—see my vanity! And dont show it: I cant remember now how bad it is; but I know it will have to be re-written in six months; and I shant do it" (*L1*, 304). Furious to learn that Violet had shared the work with their friends Ella and Walter Crum (who make a brief and not altogether flattering appearance in "The Magic Garden"), Virginia demanded the return of her draft: "You are a d—d bad woman. I asked you *not* to show my writing, and you read it to the Crums. Do send it back here at once" (*L1*, 313). She softened her appeal soon after, but insisted on reclaiming ownership of her typescript: "Will you send me back the copy of my Life of you? . . . I want to have it, great work as it is!" (*L1*, 314). Violet eventually returned the stories—after adding several handwritten suggestions of her own—and scholars have assumed that Woolf took no further interest in *The Life of Violet* after the autumn of 1907.

But the typescript I discovered in Longleat House reveals that Woolf made painstaking revisions to her mock-biography.

Despite the reluctance she had expressed to Lady Nelly—"I know it will have to be re-written in six months; and I shan't do it"—she produced an improved version and had it "copied by a Professional" (*L1*, 336). In the summer of 1908, Woolf shared the new professionally typed stories not only with Violet but also with Vanessa and Clive Bell. "Here is another of my works, written last summer," Virginia told Clive, who was fast becoming her most important literary interlocutor.[40] "It is rather thin and hasty, and as you will see, I have had to refrain and conventionalise where I might have been pointed. Even so, Violet thinks it a little harsh—such is the vanity of the modest" (*L1*, 336). But Vanessa, caring for her newborn son Julian, found nothing to apologize for in the finished version and welcomed its transgressive, liberating spirit. "I am reading your life of Violet again and really find it very witty and brilliant," she wrote to her sister, "but I wonder more and more how you ever dared to show it to her. It brings me back to the rarified culture and free talk which is so congenial to me and is a solace from talk of Julian."[41]

Vanessa's assessment of her sister's work was astute. In the metamorphosis from rough draft to finished typescript, Woolf's 1908 version of *The Life of Violet* emerged as the most fully developed, finely crafted piece of fiction she had yet written. Her revisions provide a rare glimpse into her early creative process during the period when she was learning to be her own most exacting critic, a writer bursting with literary energy whose diary, on one occasion, records dissatisfaction with her "cobblestone sentences, brisk & matter of fact, without an atom of beauty or swing about them" (*PA*, 226).[42] Each alteration Woolf made as she reworked *The Life of Violet* is telling: without adding new chapters or extensive new material to the final typescript, Woolf made hundreds of small stylistic shifts to give her draft fresh agility. We can appreciate her pursuit of a perfect sentence, each clause balanced and weighted for impact.[43] Parentheses—those innocent punctuation marks that will elasticize time and enclose devastating deaths in *To the Lighthouse*—create tonal variety and remake narrative priority. For example, parentheses added in a revision to the sentence "English society will agree that this slight but faithful conversation (there was more of it than I have quoted) is as remarkable in one way as The Ode to a Nightingale in another," yoke the narrator's curiosity-provoking omissions to Woolf's irreverence for the canon. Then Woolf, the future Hogarth Press compositor, attends to the visuality of each page, enlarging blank spaces to indicate the passage of time, narrowing and widening breaks between paragraphs to pace her stories more precisely. The sentence below concludes a paragraph in the 1907 draft, sounding like an afterthought, but Woolf turns it into a stand-alone passage in the 1908 typescript to call attention to the counterpoint between the spoken and the unspoken, the suggestive and the definitive:

> (I forgot to say that names can seldom be used in this narrative, for many are yet alive, in high places, and so on—I must beg my reader to believe that a blank means rather more than a full name, for it is capable of feeling if you guess it aright.)

And I am struck by Woolf's decision to retain her rough draft's awkward transition between the second and third chapters. Here is the end of "The Magic Garden":

> It would take me at least two more chapters to write out the significance of the place in the life of the time; how vows uttered in secret came fluttering down from the eaves of the house and settled on unexpectant heads; how odd half thoughts born in the Somersetshire school room, growing

> by fits and London drawing rooms, hospitals and streets fixed on other people and started eddies in their blood, which drove them to all kinds of unforeseen experiences, but it all goes to prove that the life of Miss Violet Dickinson is one of the most singular as well as the most prolific and least notorious that was lived in our age.
>
> In Japan they have a story fast becoming a myth, which mothers tell good children as a treat, or sick children who cannot sleep at night. Mine of course is but the English version, and all the delicate rose pinks and silvers are rubbed off it, as a schoolboy's thumb will obliterate the wing of a Peach Blossom Moth. But this is how it goes.

Woolf catches us off guard: The Japanese bedtime story—unframed by a page break or transitional phrase—inexplicably follows valedictory remarks about Violet. What might appear as draft-level haste in the violet-inked 1907 typescript emerges as deliberate artistry in the final 1908 version: an ending metamorphoses into a beginning, and Woolf invites the reader to imagine connections that the narrator withholds.

Notably, Woolf's revisions also included adopting a number of Violet Dickinson's penciled edits, which, scattered across the three stories, offered language by turns more precise, comical, or sophisticated than Woolf's own. Such instances make this mock-biography a feminist collaboration unique in Woolf's oeuvre. It was Violet who named the butcher's first child "Violus" in "Friendships Gallery" and whose marginal annotation "Lucretius 5th Book" identifies the unattributed quotation "thin jacket which grasshoppers shed in spring." In an early scene when young Violet, upbraided by Fräulein Müller for failing to understand the "History-Comedy Tragedy-Romantico-Psychology of Shakespeare," feels "that the whole of life became *intolerable*" (emphasis mine), Woolf has amplified her tradition-trapped protagonist's despair by substituting Dickinson's Latinate "intolerable" for her own original draft word "unbearable." Dickinson's influence is also imprinted on a crucial late-night dialogue between Nelly and Violet in "The Magic Garden":

> "Do you know it seems to me - well don't you think Violet - it would be very nice—-"
>
> "To have a cottage of one's own? Yes, my good woman," *cried* Violet. (emphasis mine)

Adopting Dickinson's suggestion "cried" in place of her own jarring verb "shrieked," Woolf imparts a profundity to an utterance that, as the narrator of *The Life of Violet* declares, sparks "the beginning of the great revolution which is making England a very different place from what it was," and that marks the origin of Woolf's immeasurably influential feminist phrase "a room of one's own." Read together, differences between the drafts and the finished stories are revelatory, time-stamping the moment when a writer at the beginning of her career and still in the antechambers of fame found a self-assured maturity for her literary voice.

What happened to these two versions? The revised and professionally typed stories that justly drew Vanessa's admiration in 1908 (and would have caught the eye of Woolf scholars) disappeared into the cache of Violet Dickinson's papers archived in Longleat House after her death in 1948. A slim saffron-covered volume stored with Violet's writings, correspondence, and albums, the finished work published here as *The Life of Violet* has been invisible until now. In contrast, the violet-inked leatherbound 1907 first draft surfaced briefly at mid-century and caught the eye of rising stars in London's postwar publishing circles before landing in the NYPL archives.[44]

In 1955, an agency representing Violet's maternal family, the Edens, offered the 1907 draft stories to Leonard Woolf. Leonard, perhaps intuiting Virginia's original embarrassment about saving her stories ("I dont want immaturities, things torn out of time, preserved," she had told Lady Nelly), made a definitive judgment—"I certainly did not think it worth publishing"[45]—and declined to purchase the work. The stories then turned up in a London junk shop, priced at a shilling, and fell into the hands of a young Tom Maschler, the future head of the publisher Jonathan Cape and founder of the Booker Prize, who was starting out at André Deutsch. Maschler showed the stories to his colleague Francis Wyndham (the soon-to-be editor of V. S. Naipaul and Jean Rhys), who pointed out what Maschler had not realized: the item's author "Virginia Stephen" was Virginia *Woolf*.

Maschler decided not to circulate the item among senior editors at André Deutsch. Instead, he reached out to Leonard Woolf's former Hogarth Press partner, John Lehmann, who was captivated by the stories' "characteristically Virginian atmosphere of playful high spirits" (151). Lehmann brought the stories back to Leonard and sought permission to print them in the *London Magazine*, the venerable two-hundred-year-old literary periodical Lehmann had revived after the war and whose pages, he told Leonard, were an ideal place to showcase some of "Virginia's earliest known work" (ibid.). But Leonard had been carefully publishing posthumous collections of Virginia's writings and had just released *A Writer's Diary*, his highly compacted edition of Woolf's journals, to universal praise and a new burnishing of Woolf's reputation. ("What is unique about her work," W. H. Auden wrote glowingly in the pages of *The New Yorker*, "is the combination of this mystical vision with the sharpest possible sense for the concrete, even in its humblest form."[46]) Unmoved by his former partner's enthusiasm for *The Life of Violet,* Leonard maintained that the work was only "a kind of private joke, and not very good" (151). On learning that Leonard had refused permission to publish, Maschler subsequently returned the volume to the Dickinson estate and it was acquired, along with writings, photos, and albums by Violet, by the NYPL.[47] It became part of the Virginia Woolf Papers in the Berg Collection, catalogued under Violet's title, "Friendship's Gallery."[48]

Leonard was not alone in his assessment of Virginia's drafts. The first versions of "Friendships Gallery," "The Magic Garden," and "A Story to Make You Sleep" have attracted surprisingly little critical attention. In 1979, a scholar named Ellen Hawkes came upon the draft stories in the NYPL's Berg Collection and transcribed and annotated them for a special "Virginia Woolf" issue of *Twentieth Century Literature*. The rough quality of the Berg drafts—indeterminate sentences, typographical ambiguities, unclear handwritten edits—gave Hawkes's transcription a necessarily approximate nature that has perhaps deterred Woolf scholars from taking the stories seriously; they hover on the periphery of Woolf scholarship, netting an occasional mention in the context of Violet and Virginia's relationship. (The stories do not even appear in Susan Dick's *Complete Shorter Fiction of Virginia Woolf,* a collection that includes several significantly less developed literary fragments that Woolf wrote between 1905 and 1909.[49]) Stuart Clarke included Hawkes's transcription in volume 6 of *The Essays of Virginia Woolf,* which was also published in 1979; he provided a detailed introduction and notes for the stories but relegated them to an appendix titled "Draft Essays."[50] It is charming, and perhaps a testament to *The Life of Violet*'s generic mystique, that a work declaring its own appendix "missing" wound up as an appendix within a volume not of stories but essays!

FIG. 9. Virginia Woolf (*right*), photographed with Violet Dickinson, 1902. Image source credit: Granger.

Although Virginia Woolf wrote *The Life of Violet* a full decade before her first experimental short stories, this work is not a pale version of what she would later achieve in rich, brilliant color but evidence of a career shaped from the outset by feminist commitments, humor, and determination to breathe new life into literary forms. Above all, Woolf's three-part mock-biography pays tribute to the transformative possibilities of women's friendships. As characters in "Friendships Gallery" exult, "'I too have a fire within me.' 'I too sing a delightful song.' And 'My God, I can write!' such were the sparks that spurted from Duchess and kitchen maid when Violet struck them," I hope that readers encountering these comical tales will also find themselves "struck" by Violet Dickinson, a woman whose life and writings inspired one of Virginia Woolf's most memorable characters. And because the serendipitous discovery of a revered writer's work is an occasion for joy, I also hope that readers, like the rough-spoken gardener in "The Magic Garden," will feel "excited as though something long suppressed were now rising into daylight." Can Virginia Woolf make us laugh? Of course she can.

ACKNOWLEDGMENTS

I WISH to thank the Marquess of Bath, Longleat, for permission to access his copy of "Friendship's Gallery," and Emma Challinor, Longleat House archivist, for her help with the papers of Violet Dickinson. Carolyn Vega, curator of the Henry W. and Albert A. Berg Collection of English and American Literature at the New York Public Library, offered invaluable expertise over several years; I am also grateful to Julie Carlsen and Simi Best for their help with Berg Collection materials. My thanks to Rose Lock and Philippa Murnaghan at The Keep, Sussex; Laura Walker at the British Library; Patricia McGuire at Kings College, Cambridge University; Graeme Edwards at Somerset Heritage Centre and the South West Heritage Trust; Elizabeth Mence in the Mayor's Office of the City of Bath; Nicola Beauman at Persephone Books; Jane Groufsky at Auckland Museum, New Zealand; Will Gregg at the Manuscripts Library, Washington State University; and Stephen Mielke at the Harry Ransom Center, University of Texas, Austin.

Research for *The Life of Violet* was supported by the New York Public Library, the American Philosophical Society, the National Endowment for the Humanities, the Harry Ransom Center, the Robert B. Silvers Foundation, and the Five College Consortium. I am grateful for a Benjamin Meaker Distinguished Visiting Professorship at the University of Bristol. At the University of Tennessee, Knoxville, I was privileged to receive support from the Denbo Center for Humanities & the Arts, the Hodges Better English Fund, the College of Arts and Sciences, and the Office of Research, Innovation, and Economic Development. I am especially indebted to Allen Dunn and Misty Anderson in the Department of English and to Amy Elias in the Denbo Center for Humanities & the Arts. A shout-out to Katie Bradshaw and Isabelle Alexander for research assistance, and heartfelt thanks for the tireless administrative labors of Judith Welch, Leanne Hinkle, and Molly Johnson.

It was my honor to work with Anne Savarese at Princeton University Press, and I thank her for her astute, insightful reading and enthusiasm for Woolf's stories. Thanks to Terri O'Prey and Cathryn Slovensky for editorial support. This book is wiser because of suggestions from three anonymous readers. I am grateful to the Virginia Woolf Estate and the Society of Authors, Longleat House, and Penguin Random House for permission to reproduce Woolf's typescript.

I am profoundly grateful to the friends and colleagues who shared my joy at discovering an early typescript by Virginia Woolf: Jhumpa Bhaduri, Julie Braude, Katy Chiles, Sarah Cole, Margaret Dean, Anne Fernald, Jesse Ford, Bill Hardwig, Heather Hirschfeld, Clara Jones, Rowena Kennedy-Epstein, Lisa Morrison, Vladimir Protopopescu, Paul Saint-Amour, Lisi Schoenbach, Rishona Zimring. Thanks to my parents, Bala and Girish Seshagiri, and to Chandran Seshagiri, Ilana Brownstein, and Bhaskar. There are no words expressive enough for Arjun Shankar's unstinting love. And to Jaya, Rama, and Krishna, thank you for being my best readers.

Mari Inagami (1966–2024) left the world before *The Life of Violet* entered it. Like Virginia Woolf's heroine, Mari planted beautiful gardens, loved reading, told enchanting stories about Japan, and, most of all, welcomed an ever-widening circle of friends into her home. This book is for her.

EXPLANATORY NOTES

1

Friendships Gallery

Somerset: A county in southwest England whose largest city is Bath.

Manor house: A mansion or large country house occupied by the lord or owner of an estate.

Foot rule: That is, a twelve-inch ruler.

A reason to be told in the appendix: In the draft typescript, Woolf has annotated this phrase and handwritten "this is missing" in the margin, perhaps a tongue-in-cheek joke about a lost appendix.

Font: In a church, a large freestanding stone vessel or receptacle holding consecrated water and used for baptisms.

Lycidas: The tragic title figure of a 1637 classical pastoral elegy by the English poet John Milton (1608–74), Lycidas is a virtuous young man whose drowning death halts his aspirations of joining the clergy.

A matter of conjecture: Woolf refers here to the English essayist Charles Lamb's (1775–1834) "Oxford in the Long Vacation" (1820), in which the author describes the shock of disillusionment he experienced on seeing Milton's manuscript for *Lycidas* in the Library of Trinity College, Cambridge University:

> I had thought of Lycidas as of a full-grown beauty—as springing up with all its parts absolute—till, in an evil hour, I was shown the original copy of it. [. . .] How it staggered me to see the fine things in their ore! interlined, corrected! as if their words were mortal, alterable, displaceable at pleasure! as if they might have been otherwise, and just as good! as if inspiration was made up of parts, and these fluctuating, successive, indifferent!

The reference anticipates a catalyzing early moment in Woolf's *A Room of One's Own* (1929) when the female narrator recalls Lamb's essay while walking across university grounds and decides to see Milton's *Lycidas* manuscript for herself. However, she cannot enter "that famous library where the treasure is kept" because she is a woman without a man to accompany her.

Her mother: Emily Dulcibella Eden (1833–93), Violet Dickinson's mother, was the daughter of Mary and Robert Eden, 3rd Baron of Auckland (a descendant of Edward III, Plantagenet king). Emily's paternal uncle, George Eden, 1st Earl of Auckland (1784–1849), for whom Auckland, New Zealand, was named, served as the governor-general of India. Emily's paternal aunt, Emily Eden (1797–1869), was a well-known travel writer, painter, poet, and novelist whose letters Violet Dickinson edited and published in 1919.

Hollyhock: A flowering ornamental garden plant that can grow to be nine feet tall. Victorian floriography associated hollyhocks with female ambition.

Bath Corn Exchange: The Bath Cornmarket was a long, narrow stone and brick structure erected in 1855 for merchants to trade grain. The word "corn" would have referred to any cereal or grain.

Her aunt, who was also her godmother: Perhaps an amalgam of Violet's maternal aunts, Florence Selina Eden (1835–1909) and Maria Harriet Eden (1836–1909), who never married and lived together from 1881 until their deaths.

William Penn: Woolf's mischievous falsehoods about the Dickinson family refer to Violet's Quaker ancestor Jonathan Dickinson (1663–1722), who voyaged from Jamaica to Philadelphia in 1696 to meet fellow Quaker and founder of Pennsylvania, William Penn (1644–1718). Jonathan published a dramatic account of his ten-month journey, *God's Protecting Providence, Man's Surest Help and Defence in Times of Greatest Difficulty* in 1699; Violet authored and illustrated a preface for it in the 1930s.

Virtues above rubies: From Proverbs 31.10–12 (KJV): "Who can find a virtuous woman? For her price is far above rubies. The heart of her husband doth safely trust in her, so that he shall have no need of spoil."

Squire: In the Middle Ages, a wellborn young man who attended a knight on the path to knighthood himself; by the nineteenth century, a member of the nobility.

Peer: A member of the peerage, or class of hereditary nobility. A peer might be (in descending order of importance) a duke, marquess, earl, viscount, or baron.

Recognise: to accept the authority of or show formal appreciation for something.

"Finish": to perfect or complete someone's education.

Elizabethan age: Elizabeth I (1533–1603), daughter of Henry VIII and Anne Boleyn, was queen of England and Ireland from

1558–1603. The "Virgin Queen" never married and wore **pearls** as a symbol of her chastity. English legend has it that the explorer and poet Sir Walter Raleigh (1552–1618) **put down his cloak** in front of Queen Elizabeth so that she would not have to step in mud.

Renaissance: The movement to revive classical traditions in art and culture that originated in fourteenth-century Italy and spread through most of Europe until the end of the sixteenth century.

Keats: John Keats (1795–1821), English Romantic poet who died of tuberculosis in Rome at the age of twenty-five and whose works, especially his odes, influenced subsequent generations of poets.

Wordsworth: William Wordsworth (1770–1850), English Romantic poet and poet laureate of the United Kingdom (1843–50) whose *Lyrical Ballads* (1702) was published anonymously with his fellow Romantic poet, Samuel Taylor Coleridge (1772–1834) and inaugurated a new era of English poetry emphasizing the individual artist's freedom and reverence for nature. Wordsworth's **"Ode to Duty"** (1805) is a seven-stanza poem whose speaker addresses the titular virtue, "Stern Daughter of the Voice of God!"

Her first season: The London social season coincided with the sitting of Parliament from late January to July. A young woman's "first season" marked her formal entrance into society and announced her eligibility for marriage on the basis of age, education, beauty, and accomplishments.

Gladstone's ministry: William Ewart Gladstone (1809–98), four-time prime minster of England, whose terms ran from 1868–74, 1880–85, 1886, and 1892–94.

Grizzle: To turn gray-haired.

Ode to a Nightingale: John Keats's influential 1819 eight-stanza ode on mortality, nature, dreams, and song. The line **"truth is beauty"** hails not from this poem but from Keats's "Ode on a Grecian Urn" (1819).

Enteric: Another name for typhoid.

Good Samaritan: A reference to Luke 10:25–37, where Jesus tells the story of a Samaritan who stopped to help a man who had been robbed, beaten, and stripped of his clothes. The phrase "good Samaritan" generally refers to a kind, helpful individual.

Winds of heaven: A biblical phrase referring to east, west, north, and south winds.

Costermonger: One who sells fruit or vegetables from a street cart.

Investigated: That is, their lineage was traced precisely.

"Thin jacket which grasshoppers shed in spring": A line translated from the Roman philosopher Lucretius's didactic poem *De rerum natura,* or *On the Nature of Things* (ca. 50 BC): "Folliculos ut nunc teretis aestate cicadae / Lincunt sponte sua victum vitamque petentes" (V.ll.803–4). Woolf mentions reading Lucretius in two 1907 letters to Violet Dickinson. Violet penciled "Lucretius 5th Book" next to this line in the margin of the 1907 draft typescript. In the professionally typed Longleat version, Woolf penned an asterisk after the quote and copied Violet's note in the margin.

Instincticise: A word of Woolf's invention.

Irish grandmother: Violet's paternal grandmother, Sophia Smith (1784–1844), was English, not Irish; her grandfather,

William Dickinson (1771–1837), was a member of Parliament, and not, as Woolf teasingly declares, **"a North country spinner,"** meaning someone employed to spin thread or yarn from fibers.

Loch Ness: A lake in the Scottish Highlands.

Elijah: Old Testament Hebrew prophet who parted the River Jordan by striking it with his mantle and who subsequently ascended to heaven in a chariot of fire drawn by horses of fire. See Kings 2.2.

"Och Och Ochone!": An Irish or Scottish exclamation of sorrow or regret.

Throstle: A water- or steam-powered spinning machine for cotton or wool invented in the late eighteenth century, not by Violet's grandfather but by the entrepreneurial Lancashire industrialist Richard Arkwright (1732–92).

Bans: Bans, or more commonly, banns, are the public announcement of an upcoming marriage made by a parish church.

Marriage settlements: A broad term encompassing diverse legal arrangements for the transfer and inheritance of property upon marriage.

Lancashire rods of steel: Lancashire, a major industrial center in northwest England, was the site of collieries, ironworks, and steelworks.

2

The Magic Garden

'bus: Short for omnibus, originally a horse-drawn London conveyance replaced by motorized buses by 1905.

Jumping Elephant: A Westminster locale of Woolf's invention, not to be confused with Elephant and Castle in Southwark.

Royal Academicians: King George III (1738–1820) founded the Royal Academy of Arts in London in 1768, and the painter Sir Joshua Reynolds (1723–92) served as its first president. Royal Academicians are a highly select group of eighty practicing painters, printmakers, architects, and sculptors who teach at the Royal Academy Schools and hold their positions until the age of seventy-five.

No. 25: Violet Dickinson has annotated this as "Grove End Road," which was Lady Nelly and Lord Robert Cecil's address in London. Grove End Road in St. Johns Wood (*see below*) was home to numerous artists.

Chow dog: A medium-sized dog with a soft, dense coat, originally from Northern China.

Fritillaries: Woolf might refer here to a member of the lily family, *Fritillaria,* whose bell-shaped flowers have a checkered pattern, or to fritillary butterflies, *Nymphalidae,* which have orange and black checkered wings.

Freaked with jet: "Freaked" means streaked or spotted at random; "jet" means glossy black. The phrase "freak'd with jet" appears in Milton's *Lycidas*:

> Bring the rathe primrose that forsaken dies,
> The tufted crow-toe, and pale jessamine,
> The white pink, and the pansy freak'd with jet,
> The glowing violet,
> The musk-rose, and the well attir'd woodbine,
> With cowslips wan that hang the pensive head,

And every flower that sad embroidery wears;
Bid amaranthus all his beauty shed,
And daffadillies fill their cups with tears,
To strew the laureate hearse where Lycid lies.

Violet has written in the margins "? Pansies only," next to this paragraph, suggesting that she has *Lycidas* in mind.

Within the pages of Burke: Burke's Peerage Limited, a publishing house founded by the genealogist John Burke (1786–1848) in 1826 and still in existence today, produced numerous ancestral and genealogical volumes about distinguished families. Their first publication was *A General and Heraldic Dictionary of the Peerage and Baronetage of the United Kingdom for MDCCCXXVI. Exhibiting, under strict alphabetical arrangement, The Present State of those exalted Ranks, with their Armorial Bearings, Mottoes, etc., And deducing the Lineage of each House from the Founder of its Honors.*

Free trader: One who supported reciprocal trade between Britain and its colonies and an opponent of **protectionist gain**, or the profits secured by imposing tariffs on foreign goods to protect domestic industries from foreign competition. Kitty Maxse's husband, the Conservative writer and editor Leo Maxse, was a protectionist who supported the powerful statesman **Joseph Chamberlain**'s (1836–1914) proposals for tariff reform.

Darwin: Charles Darwin (1809–82), the British naturalist who revolutionized science with his theories of evolution and natural selection. The best-known of his many books are *On the Origin of Species by Means of Natural Selection* (1859) and *The Descent of Man* (1871).

Valetudinarian: An invalid or person in poor health.

St. Johns Wood: A residential Westminster suburb northwest of Regent's Park, St. Johns Wood is the site of Lord's Cricket Ground and was home to several writers, painters, sculptors, and architects in the late nineteenth and early twentieth centuries.

***Lloyd's Weekly*:** A Sunday paper established in London in 1842, *Lloyd's Weekly Newspaper* reported domestic and foreign news; its pages also featured fiction, poetry, and arts coverage generally. *Lloyd*'s readership of men and women in the UK and abroad (especially in Australia and New Zealand) crossed one million in 1896; circulation peaked at 1.5 million during World War I. The newspaper ceased publication in 1931.

Charwoman: A part-time housekeeper who earns daily wages by tidying and doing other household tasks.

Kippered herrings: An inexpensive staple of British breakfast and high tea from the Victorian era through most of the twentieth century, "kippers," as they are informally known, are slices of whole herring that have been salted and smoked.

Cutlets: Also called chops, unbreaded slices of veal or mutton served fried or broiled.

Flunkeys: Condescending term for footmen or other male servants, traditionally dressed in **livery**, or uniforms, and assigned menial tasks.

Temperature tube: That is, a thermometer.

Dowager: A woman who has inherited property, title, or wealth from a deceased husband.

Green fly: Another name for *Aphidoidea*, or aphids.

Specialist: A doctor or other medical practitioner concentrating on one particular disease or system of the body.

Public house: An inn or tavern licensed to sell alcohol and generally referred to as a pub.

George Trevelyan: George Macaulay Trevelyan (1876–1962), prolific British historian, biographer, and memoirist whose *British History in the Nineteenth Century, 1782–1901* was only published in 1922 (Woolf's invented title here, "The Social Life of the Nineteenth Century," notwithstanding). In *A Room of One's Own,* Woolf alludes to Trevelyan's 1926 *History of England* in her analysis of the contrast between women in history and women in literature.

George Meredith: The Victorian novelist and poet George Meredith (1828–1909) best known for *The Ordeal of Richard Feverel* (1859), *The Egoist* (1879), and *Diana of the Crossways* (1885).

Purblind: Literally, nearly or partially blind; as a figure of speech, dimwitted or lacking discernment.

Porridge off earthenware: Oatmeal eaten from thick or rough dishes, typical of a working- or middle-class breakfast rather than a multicourse aristocratic breakfast served on bone china.

Stays: A two-pieced whalebone- or metal-stiffened underbodice worn by women to support the torso, similar to a corset.

H---d: Hatfield House, a grand Jacobean house in Hertfordshire, was built in 1611 by Robert Cecil, 1st Earl of Salisbury. Hatfield House adjoined the Old Palace of Hatfield, the residence of Henry VIII and his children Edward, Elizabeth, and Mary.

The slopes of Olympus and the Temples of Bacchus: In Greek mythology, Mount Olympus was the abode of the gods. The Temple of Bacchus, an enormous second-century Roman temple still standing in the Beqaa Valley in Lebanon, honors the god of wine.

Laurels: *Laurus nobilis,* commonly called a laurel or bay tree, is a flowering evergreen tree or shrub.

Fauns: Rural deities with the bodies of men and the horns, ears, tail, and sometimes the legs of goats.

Shillings: British coins worth twelve pence or 1/20th of a pound. Shillings stopped circulating in 1971, when they were replaced with five pence coins.

Bastille: The Paris fortress-turned-prison stormed on July 14, 1789, and a symbol of the people's victory in the French Revolution.

Pyrus Japonica: *Pieris japonica* is a flowering quince, a fruit-bearing evergreen shrub with red, white, or pink flowers.

Cyrus Asiatica: A plant of Woolf's invention, perhaps a version of *Centella asiatica* or pennywort.

Dyspepsia: Another word for indigestion.

Caustic: Sticks of silver nitrate used surgically to burn and destroy living tissue.

Phylloxera: A tiny yellow aphid-like insect that feeds on the roots of grapevines and creates significant damage to vineyards. Gardeners combat phylloxera infestation by using **paraffin**, a soft petroleum- or coal-derived wax, to graft a phylloxera-resistant grapevine with a wine grape plant.

"I dessay": I daresay.

"Moth and rust": A reference to Matthew 6:19–21 (KJV), where Jesus warns against the ephemerality and corruptibility of earthly possessions: "Lay not up for yourselves treasures upon earth, where moth and rust doth corrupt, and where thieves break through and steal: But lay up for yourselves treasures in heaven, where neither moth nor rust doth corrupt, and where thieves do not break through nor steal: For where your treasure is, there will your heart be also."

Pile: A stately building or home.

Glasshouses: Greenhouses or conservatory buildings for growing plants.

Hertfordshire: An English county northeast of London among whose ten districts was **Welwyn** (now called Welwyn Hatfield).

Copse: A thicket or grove of small trees.

Coptic scholars: Experts in the history and religious practices of Copts, Egyptian Christians whose writing, arts, and architecture bear Greco-Roman, Islamic, and Byzantine influences. Walter Crum was a Coptic scholar.

Pruning hook: A handheld gardening tool with a curved blade.

Acropolis: A citadel in Athens home to some of the most storied and architecturally influential structures of the ancient world, including the Parthenon, the temple of Nike Athena, and the Erechtheum.

British Museum: Founded in London 1753 by an Act of Parliament, the British Museum was the world's first national public museum. The Museum's Greek Revival architecture, enormous collections, and especially its famous circular Reading Room are important features in Woolf's writings; see *Jacob's Room* and *A Room of One's Own*.

Fitzroy Square: A residential square in Bloomsbury where Woolf lived from 1907–11 with her younger brother Adrian Stephen. She drafted part of her first novel, *The Voyage Out,* from her rooms in 29 Fitzroy Square.

St. Pancras: A central London parish originally served by the St. Pancras Old Church and then by the New Church after 1822.

Burnt . . . as thin as the black films of paper: Perhaps a reference to the technique of developing a photograph by "burning" or overexposing film to darken an image. Woolf was an enthusiastic amateur photographer.

Bleating, chuckling, groaning: Perhaps sounds signaling the various animal nicknames Woolf gave herself in her letters to Violet and others: "Goat," "Sparroy" (a combination of sparrow and monkey), and "Wallaby."

Adonais: "Adonais: An Elegy on the Death of John Keats," a fifty-five-stanza pastoral elegy in the tradition of Milton's *Lycidas* written in 1821 by the English Romantic poet Percy Bysshe Shelley (1792–1822).

German spa: Any one of several towns in Germany with mineral springs thought to possess curative properties for a variety of ailments.

Peach Blossom moth: *Thyatira batis,* a brown moth marked with pale pink blotches resembling peach blossoms.

3

A Story to Make You Sleep

Oriental Grebe Podicipes Oristatus: *Podiceps Cristatus,* or great crested grebe, a black-and-white aquatic diving bird.

"Tsai gun": Woolf takes the liberty of inventing and footnoting translations for an ersatz "Japanese" vocabulary in this and eight other instances in the story. None of her phrases belongs to spoken or written Japanese.

Dinted: Marked or indented with pressure or force.

Mandarin: Originally, an official in the imperial Chinese civil service; more informally, an official or authoritative figure in East Asia.

Laburnum: Sometimes called "golden rain," *Laburnum anagyroides* is a small May- and June-blooming tree with bright yellow flowers that grow in hanging bunches.

Heathens: A typically derogatory or depreciative term for non-Christian people, or, more broadly, for people of any religion whose worship practices are considered unorthodox by other members of that religion.

Emulous: Desiring to obtain by imitating; animated by the spirit of rivalry.

TEXTUAL NOTES

Revisions to Chapter 1, "Friendships Gallery"

1907 TYPESCRIPT (NYPL)	**1908 TYPESCRIPT (Longleat House)**
crying	crying,
once	once,
historian	historian,
avoided	avoided,
machine	machine,
Its	It's
Sir,	Sir,"
Nurse; if	Nurse, "if
the cleverest child the noisiest child and the child with the fine finest lungs [VW's line breaks]	the cleverest child, the noisiest child, and the child with the finest lungs [typed as one standard continuous line]
Parish	Parish,
have not	have it not,
name;	name,
God mothers	god-mothers
God fathers	god-fathers
smiled	smiled,
now	now,
skin	skin,
then;	then,
mother;	mother.
"Violet.	Violet.

eight;	eight,
room	room,
thought	thought,
prejudiced;	prejudiced,
Godmother	godmother.
Dickinson,	Dickinson,"
Goodness	goodness
grow;	grow,
Godliness." The	Godliness. [new ¶] The
Dickinsons	Dickinson's
you"	you,"
ME." Then	ME. [new ¶] Then
Nieces	niece's
evening. Mary	evening. [new ¶] Mary
society	society,
too	too,
in short it was agreed	it was agreed
opinions;	opinions
Crosses;	Crosses,
"G's	"G's"
them. And	them; and
growin	growing
attention,	attention --
title.; the	title; and
it. When	it. [new ¶] When
Emblem	emblem
before. But	before; but
indivisible;	indivisible,
Fraülein Müller	Fraulein Muller
melodramatic	melodramatic,

particular	particular,
Drama;	drama.
Fraülein	Fraulein
Comedy Tragedy	Comedy-Tragedy
credit Mademoiselle	credit, Mademoiselle,
Bath!"	Bath."
~~unbearable~~ [Violet handwrites "intolerable"]	intolerable [Violet's edit]
Violet,	Violet.
drama"	drama,"
credit. "But	credit. [new ¶] "But
But. . . . . " Human	But. . . . . " -- Human
saying	saying,
humanity.	humanity;
deal;	deal,
internally	internally,
fathers	father's
schoolroom	schoolroom,
exclaimed;	exclaimed,
paper;	paper,
begin Her first Season [Violet handwrites "with" and marks for insertion before "Her"]	begin with her first season [VW adds Violet's "with"; she changes case and does not make this a stand-alone line]
birth parentage education	birth, parentage, education,
that	that,
flower	flower,
it; [the rest of this page is blank]	it, [end of a paragraph, page continues with the next paragraph]
Violets [start of a new page]	Violet's
has	has,
doubt	doubt,

Lady ______ ________. (I forgot	Lady . . . . [new ¶] (I forgot
on;	on ---
name	name,
trunk;	trunk,
Oh	Oh,
'i'" went	'i'," went
think,	think
tickled;	tickled,
laughing"	laughing,"
say;	say,
Whats your name	Whats-your-name
it.	it,
behind?"	behind,"
Lady ------- ------	Lady. . . . .
Most	"Most
know -- One	know. One
streets;	streets,
bath --	bath,
church	church,
rose;	rose,
Tuesday--Wednesday, to	Tuesday? - Wednesday? to
conversation; there quoted	conversation (there quoted)
is	[deleted]
heart;	heart,
caverns	caverns,
Lord. . . . .;	Lord . . . .
cess pool "enough whiffs"	cesspool. "Enough whiffs,"
Dr	Dr.
soapsuds "the	soapsuds -- "the
life" while	life" -- while
butchers	butcher's
after noon	afternoon

Vioelnt [Violet handwrites "Violent" and above that "Violus"]	Violus
church	church,
Ass	Ass,
me" "I	me." "I
song" and	song." And
"My, God	"My God!
write!" -- such	write!" such
down;	down,
honey combs	honey-combs
friends --	friends,
me	me,
'g's	"g's"
'hs'	"h's"
grandmother;	grandmother,
cloud shapes	cloud-shapes
pit --	pit,
other;	other,
beasts	beasts,
God	God,
Mr	Mr.

Revisions to Chapter 2, "The Magic Garden"

1907 TYPESCRIPT (NYPL)	**1908 TYPESCRIPT (Longleat House)**
Bus	'bus
No 25, --- you	No. 25 -- you
chairs;	chairs,
shoulders	shoulders,
chow	Chow
always;	always,
lawn, laces	lawn, their laces

spikes,	spikes ---
Burke. [the rest of the page is blank]	Burke. [new ¶]
for	for,
char woman	charwoman
things;	things,
pictures;	pictures,
love with life; This	love, with life. This
adore it. [rest of the page blank] [new page] But	adore it. [new ¶] But
ladies;	ladies,
Health,	health
"health"	health
mean	mean,
mean	mean,
that;	that,
Mrs M----x----e	(Mrs. M----x----e)
explain	explain,
a chart;	'a chart,'
normal; O	normal, oh!
creek	creek,
useless,	useless;
freetrader;	free trader
99!	99.
flying,	flying --
were	we're
sea,	sea --
Leo,	Leo,"
is	"is
never to lose	never lose
you -- I	you (I
wash stand --	wash stand)
alive! and	alive!" and

think" Now	think, "now
and	And
drains	drains,
is	is
connection	connection,
surprised	surprised,
St	St.
wood	Wood,
Dickinson; She	Dickinson. She
there;	there,
back;	back,
tiles;	tiles,
advise	advice
though!	though,
prose [rest of page is blank]	prose. [new ¶] She,
When	When,
back	back,
really	~~really~~
"The social	"The Social
spirit	spirit,
and	and,
laughed;	laughed,
on	on,
notes	notes,
how	~~how~~
quantities	quantities,
sex	sex,
describe then	describe, then,
H------d,	H----d
scales	scales,"
Violet	Violet,
scene;	scene,
there	~~there~~

them whence	them, whence,
moment	moment,
creature;	creature,
bushes;	bushes --
fauns;	fauns,
picture --	picture,
day"	day,"
lady;	lady,
man	man,
spoke;	spoke,
earth	earth,
body;	body,
manure;	manure,
apology	apology,
wifes	wife's
caustic	'caustic
tumours	tumours'
how	the way
dessay." [rest of the page is blank]	dessay." [new ¶]
Violet	Violet,
indoors	indoors,
discontent	discontent;
beautiful	beautiful,
stones	stones,
not	not,
perceive	perceive,
selfishness	selfishness,
confusions;	confusions,
also	also,
genius	genius,
tones	tones,
herself	herself,
suffocated;	suffocated,

pay	pay,
smoothness;	smoothness,
feel	feel,
air. [rest of the page is blank]	air. [new ¶]
revolution;	revolution,
anchor.	anchor --
wall	wall --
this;	this --
said	said,
change;	change,
was	were
Can	"Can
me	me,"
where	"where
out	out,
Cookson?" "Is	Cookson?" "[new ¶] Is
laughing,	laughing;
ladies	lady's
honour"	honour,"
onc	one's
woman	woman,"
~~shrieked~~ [Violet strikes out and writes "cried" above]	cried
in	in,
ancestors"	ancestors,"
tall	tall,
play;	play,
road	road,
air;	air,
say;	say,
notes,	notes;
on the her knee	on her knees

asked; here	asked. Here
been;	been,
Cottage;	Cottage
gone. But	gone -- but
fellows;	fellows,
pruned	pruned,
mistress. serving	mistress, serving
country;	country,
C---l, it	C----l (it
ear,	ear)
Fauns. [rest of page is blank]	Fauns. [new ¶]
given	given,
solicitudes;	solicitudes
world	worlds
if one	if indeed one
was	were
it;	it,
cottage;	cottage,
front;	front,
exclaim "No body	exclaim. "Nobody
me;	me,
weed;	weed,
yes,	yes
fairly;	fairly.
truth and one	truth and -- one
thing;	thing,
O yes	Oh yes,
one two three four five	one, two, three, four, five
Brambles"	Brambles,
virtues;	virtues,
tree (Oak beech sycamore?)	tree ~~(Oak beech sycamore?)~~
prose;	prose,
women;	women,

woman;	woman,
and	and,
picture --	picture,
course	course,
aesthetics;	aesthetics,
mistakenly,	unmistakeably, [*sic*]
like" and	like", and
them	them,
eyes	eyes,
shapes	shapes,
texts	texts,
hospital	hospital,
tears,	tears
say	say,
ointment." how	ointment" -- how
done	done,
remain	remain,
bewilderment;	bewilderment,
till	till,
depths	depths,
for	~~for~~
heads;	heads,
rooms	rooms,
street	streets
blood	blood,
experiences;	experiences,
story,	story

Revisions to Chapter 3, "A Story to Make You Sleep"

1907 TYPESCRIPT (NYPL)	**1908 TYPESCRIPT (Longleat House)**
time	time,
ancestors;	ancestors,

behold! -- the	behold! the
devils	devils,
chin-chins* egg	chin-chin's egg[x]
thousand	thousands
children; Behold	children, behold
world;	world,
days,	Days,
him;	him --
them;	them,
Gun;[1]	Gun,"[x]
Gun[2]"	Gun,"[xx]
Gun[3];	Gun".[xxx]
know	know,
him	him,
world;	world,
pated	Pated
city;	city,
flame;	flame,
prayed	prayed,
hail;	hail,
together;	together,
away"	away,"
homes"	homes."
one	one,
priest	Priest
so;	so,
saying,	saying.
windows -- many	windows (many
mountains	mountains,
left -- they	left) they
Rick-Shi*	Rick-Shi[x]
today.	to-day.

barley; [page break]	barley, [no page break]
swish;	swish,
lower;	lower,
mother-in-law	mothers-in-law
kinsmen. and	kinsmen, and
pray they	pray and they
Behold! the	behold! The
since I	since -- I
garments;	garments,
crows;	crows,
stairs; They	stairs. They
brim;	brim,
bird nest	birds nest
heads	heads,
crane	crane,
worship;	worship,
God	God,
could;	could,
Rim, Shi-ki[1]	Rim Shi-Ki[x]
growing;	growing,
too	too,
height;	height,
her;	her,
beasts;	beasts,
shoots; she	shoots. She
offering, here	offering there
water;	water,
here	there
aright;	aright,
weave magic spells	weave spells
how	how,
apples	apples,

sheep. [page break]	sheep [no page break]
Baths; answered	Baths." answered
Rim Shi Ki	Rim-Shi-Ki
moment; that	moment, "That
best;	best,
Sin Sin	[x]Sin Sin
house; it.	house. It
wall the	wall and the
figures,	figures
naked;	naked,
a hand	hand
up	up,
exception	exception,
happy	happy,
healthy	healthy,
rich	rich,
bath"	bath,"
old"	old,"
"Babes" All	"Babes." [new ¶] All
of	of,
corner;	corner,
crust	crust,
died;	died,
Tokio"	Tokio."
time;	time,
Princesses;	Princesses,
stand;	stand,
Tokio;	Tokio,
Monster;	Monster,
other;	other,
Heathens. for	Heathens. For
her;	her,

with	with,
virtue;	virtue,
you	you,
Mayor;	Mayor,
honours	crowns
Garden;	Garden,
whispers,	whispers
Moon;	Moon,
Japan;	Japan,
prophecies. [page break]	prophecies. [no page break]
conceivable; by	conceivable. By
moon shine	moonshine
them;	them,
sun;	sun,
two."	two" ----
waves;	waves,
hilltop;	hilltop,
settled;	settled,
fruit	fruit,
underclothing	underclothing,
one;	one,
books	books,
lit;	lit,
night;	night
another	Another
Power,	Power
name.	name?
night	night,
Bats;	Bats,
opinion;	opinion.
me, he	me," he
night, that	night, "that

laughter;	laughter,
dormice;	dormice --
Goddesses;	goddesses --
likely he said	likely," he said
you	"you
angrily since the	angrily, "the
Owl	owl
laughter, or,	laughter or
moon;	moon,
true, said	true," said
people; But	people." But
Most Gods	Gods
offerings;	offerings,
so said	so," said
gentleman, but	gentleman, "but
Goddesses	goddesses
any thing	anything
theirs;	theirs,
live;	live,
so on;	so on,
other [page break]	other. [no page break]
odd, --	odd,
anothers wife	another's wife
said;	said,
mistaken. [no paragraph break]	mistaken. [new ¶]
on	upon
snake;	snake,
graves.; now	graves and now
the	a
top;	top,
off in	off him in

ant like	ant-like
town,	town
globe;	globe,
back;	back,
Princesses;	Princesses,
again"	again."
hours;	hours --
story;	story,
into	in
embroider. and	embroidery, and

NOTES TO THE AFTERWORD

1. Carlyle, *On Heroes*, 45.

2. On the details of Violet and Virginia's friendship, see Briggs, *Virginia Woolf: An Inner Life*; Curtis and Briggs, *Virginia Woolf's Women*; Forrester, *Virginia Woolf: A Portrait*; Gordon, *Virginia Woolf: A Writer's Life*; King, *Virginia Woolf*; Lee, *Virginia Woolf*; and Rudikoff, *Ancestral Houses*. Also see Cook, "'Women Alone Stir My Imagination,'" for a discussion of this friendship in the context of the obstacles facing feminist scholars in the twentieth century who sought to expand academic discourse about modern women writers.

3. Somerset Heritage Centre, *Manuscript History of the Dickinson Family*, vol. 2, 1940, reference number DD/DN/5/6/3 (120); subsequent references to this source are given by reference and page number in the main text and notes.

4. See Burden, *Winging Westward*.

5. *The Letters of Virginia Woolf*, vol. 6, 158; subsequent references to the *Letters* are given as *L* followed by the volume number and page number (if there is one).

6. Violet's brooch replicates the mayor's seal and represents Bath's city walls and portcullis in rubies, emeralds, pearls, and enamelwork. It is displayed in a glass case alongside other historically significant items in the Mayor's Parlour in the Guildhall of the City of Bath.

7. See Spielmann and Layard, *The Life and Work of Kate Greenaway*.

8. Woolf recalled this convalescence in "Old Bloomsbury," a 1922 piece for the Bloomsbury Memoir Club: "I had lain in bed at the Dickinsons' house at Welwyn thinking that the birds were singing Greek choruses and that King Edward was using the foulest possible language among Ozzie Dickinson's azaleas" (184).

9. *These Thoughts Were Written By Anthony Harte*, p. 1. Violet, apparently an amateur bookbinder, had initially sent Virginia a faultily made copy of the booklet. "Please inscribe and send me another copy of Anthony Harte, as my copy is all wrongly bound, and numbered, and the same pages are repeated," Virginia requested, praising her friend: "I think them excellent however in spite of this drawback" (*L1*,

postcard, January 1905, 174–75). The corrected version bears Violet's inscription, "A Tract for The Sp[arroy]: Fr. V.D. 1905," and is archived in the Washington State University Library.

10. *A Passionate Apprentice*, 221 and 9; subsequent references to this source are hereafter given in the main text and notes as *PA* followed by the page number.

11. *These Thoughts Were Written By Anthony Harte* resurfaced as a point of connection between Violet and Virginia in 1937. In a letter to Violet, who was recovering from a broken leg, Woolf wrote: "[Y]our heart is the purest unfractured gold. I was led to make these foolish remarks by tidying my bookcase: and out fell a very small red book, in which you wrote A Tract for the Sp: fr. V.D. 1905. Now when so much has gone down the sink, see how affectionate I must be, and admiring of your writers gift [. . .] to have kept that and still read it after 32 years!" (*L1*, 184).

12. Violet describes these doings in essays and stories archived as "Unpublished Items from the Violet Dickinson Collection, Longleat."

13. Captain Humphrey-Davies correspondence, collection of Auckland War Memorial Museum - Tāmaki Paenga Hira. MUS-1995-42-11.

14. Violet wrote numerous short pieces about subjects such as London neighborhoods, encounters with strangers, her touching relationship with a family of dwarfs in Manchester Street, and new innovations in crematorium technology.

15. Jonathan Dickinson, for whom a state park is named in Martin County, Florida, originally gave his memoir the astonishing title *God's Protecting Providence, man's surest help and defence, in times of the greatest difficulty, and most eminent danger: evidenced in the remarkable deliverance of Robert Barrow, with divers other persons, from the devouring waves of the sea; amongst which they suffered shipwrack: and also, from the cruel, devouring jaws of the inhumane canibals of Florida* [1700]. Violet's twenty-two-page preface for this work, authored in the 1930s, includes a family tree, hand-drawn and colored maps, and portraits of William Penn and his father.

16. These volumes include original manuscripts and artwork and were purchased at auction from Christie's in 2022. Their present whereabouts are unknown.

17. Emily Eden published a volume of her lithographs called *Portraits of the Princes & People of India* in 1844 (the original paintings now hang in the Victoria Memorial Museum in Calcutta). Her novels *The Semi-Detached House* (1859) and *The Semi-Attached Couple* (1860) were likened to Jane Austen's. She also published *Up the Country: Letters Written to Her Sister from the Upper Provinces of India* (1867), an account of two years of traveling through India in the company of her brother George Eden, Baron of Auckland, then governor-general of India. In 1983, *Up the Country* was one of the first titles reprinted by the pioneering English feminist publisher, Virago Press, for the Virago Travellers series.

18. Woolf wrote to Violet praising *Miss Eden's Letters* as "one of the best collections for ever so long," a sentiment echoed in her *Times Literary Supplement* review

"Real Letters": "The judgment of Miss Dickinson's selections and the unusual excellence of her materials give the book what we so seldom find in biographies—construction and artistic purpose" (122).

19. See *L6*, 89.

20. On Violet's objection to Bloomsbury, see *L1*, 283–87. Violet's biographer tells us that "in old age more peppery and more deaf," Violet spent her last years "in comfort in her Wood till she finally withered away." Somerset Heritage Centre, "Mary Violet Dickinson; 9th Generation," *Manuscript History of the Dickinson Family*, vol. 2, 1940 (DD/DN/5/6/3 [123]).

21. See, e.g., Hermione Lee in *Virginia Woolf*: "Violet enabled [Virginia] to behave freely, childishly, like a daughter or a favourite pet or a sweetheart. She was devoted, interested, and without aggression. She provided a space in which Virginia could curl up or hurl herself about, and be as egotistical and demanding as her dying father" (169).

22. *Early Writings by Virginia Stephen* (ca. 1902), in *Monks House Papers: Papers of Virginia Woolf and Related Papers of Leonard Woolf*, University of Sussex Library, reference number SxMs-18-2-A-26.74. Subsequent references to this source are given by reference and page number in the main text and notes.

23. For example, Virginia sent Violet a comic biography of her paternal aunt, Caroline Emilia Stephen (this work, unfortunately, has been lost) that drew Violet's admiration. Vanessa wrote to her sister that Violet was "simply full of your praises" and "thinks your writing most wonderful": "She said she had sat and howled over the life of Caroline Emilia. [. . .] She thought you would undoubtedly be a great writer one day. Your things are so well thought out—fresh and original and interesting. Is that enough for you? She really thinks you a genius." Bell and Marler, *Selected Letters of Vanessa Bell*, Dec. 7, 1904, 27.

24. Between 1904 and 1907, Woolf's signed and unsigned writings appeared in *The Guardian*, *Times Literary Supplement*, *National Review*, *Academy and Literature*, and *Speaker*. See Andrew McNeillie, introduction to *The Essays of Virginia Woolf*, vol. 1 (London: Hogarth Press, 1986), ix–xviii.

25. Rudikoff, 89. Rudikoff's *Ancestral Houses* offers biographical details about the women who inspired the characters in *The Life of Violet*. See also Kathryn Simpson, "Friends and Lovers," in *The Oxford Handbook of Virginia Woolf*, on Woolf's lifelong friendships with women.

26. To take one example: In 1907, Woolf wrote a particularly acid letter to Lady Nelly about her Aunt Caroline and others in her circle who insisted that she prioritize marriage, suggesting that she would avenge herself through her writing: "[Y]ou dont have to contend with obscene old women, and young women too with beaks dripping gore, who advise you to marry. That is my daily penance, and has been these six months. 'I think you should keep a maid Virginia—to do your hair—it makes such

a difference—Men notice these things—not of course'- and so on and so on. Well, one of these days they shall have their paragraph—That is a terrible threat!" (296)

27. Letter to Emma Vaughan, August 23, 1901.

28. Woolf, "The Value of Laughter," in *Essays*, vol. 1, 58–60.

29. On the contest between philosophies of idealism and realism in Woolf's novels, see Ann Banfield, *The Phantom Table: Woolf, Fry, Russell and the Epistemology of Modernism.*

30. Woolf, *Three Guineas*, 16, 130, and 125.

31. This delegation's voyage was also recorded in a woman's journal: Alice Roosevelt (1884–1980), the famously boundary-breaking daughter of President Theodore Roosevelt, kept an elaborate diary-album of her experiences as a leading member of the 1905 Taft Mission's visits to Japan, the Philippines, China, and Korea. She would write about the trip in her 1933 autobiography, *Crowded Hours* (New York: Charles Scribner's Sons).

32. Violet pasted in, for example, business cards from diplomats, furriers, hoteliers, and interpreters; the ground plan of a Nagasaki hospital; a twelve-course dinner menu from the SS *Bremen* that carried the group from Colombo to Suez.

33. Violet's album, p. 13, 1905. Berg Collection, NYPL.

34. Violet did not keep a complete record of everyone she met on the trip, but among her notable traveling companions were Sir Michael Hicks Beach, Earl of St. Aldwyn, and his family (Sir Michael's daughter Susan had been the model for Britannia on coins struck by King Edward VII); Harold George Parlett, translator and scholar of Japanese Buddhism; and Sir Claude Maxwell MacDonald, first British ambassador to Japan, and his wife, Lady Ethel MacDonald.

At a dinner held at the British legation in Tokyo, Violet met Ito Hirobumi, Prime Minister of Japan and Viscount K. Tanaka, Japanese Minister of the Imperial Household. The evening is recounted in the memoirs of yet another woman diarist, Eleanora Mary, Baroness Albert d'Anethan, poet, novelist, memoirist, and sister of H. Rider Haggard. In *Fourteen Years of Diplomatic Life in Japan* (1912), Baroness d'Anethan describes her first impressions of Violet. "September 23, 1905: A dinner took place at the British Legation to meet Sir Michael and Lady Hicks-Beech [*sic*] and their two tall daughters. Lord and Lady Robert Cecil were also there. He is the late Lord Salisbury's second son. I sat between Marquis Ito and Viscount Tanaka. A[lbert] took in to dinner a Miss Dickinson, a friend of Lady Robert Cecil's. She stands 6 feet 3½ inches in her shoes, and when a little Japanese tailor measured her for a gown, she quaintly suggested the use of a ladder. She seems a very nice girl" (454–55).

35. Founded in 1841, *Punch, or the London Charivari* was a popular illustrated humorous weekly magazine. The magazine's satirical cartoons often made fun of British colonial life abroad.

36. See Gregory Irvine, *Japonisme and the Rise of the Modern Art Movement*, and Ayako Ono, *Japonisme in Britain.*

37. For example, Woolf received an invitation to a lecture by the Japanese art scholar Laurence Binyon in 1905, and her encounters with East Asian arts more broadly multiplied when the critic and artist Roger Fry entered her life. Fry's two postimpressionist exhibitions in 1910 and 1911, followed by the art objects produced in the Omega Workshops (1913–18) and his writings on form, occasioned Woolf's several reflections on how to adopt or adapt various aesthetic sensibilities from around the world into her writing. See Urmila Seshagiri, *Race and the Modernist Imagination*.

38. In a lengthy diary entry for Christmas 1904 that anticipates the *The Life of Violet*, Woolf describes the scenery of the New Forest as though it were a "floating world" in a Japanese woodblock:

> The sunset makes all the air as though of melted amethyst; yellow flakes dissolve from the solid body of amethyst which is the west. Against this, standing as though in an ocean of fine air, the bare trees are deep black lines, as though drawn in Indian ink which has dried dull and indelible. The small branches & twigs make a fringe of infinitely delicate lines, each one distinctly cut against the sky. . . . The trees have green velvet jackets of moss. This the brightest colour in the landscape. A peach bloom of silver & plum colour covers the trees at a little distance. Also a pale green lichen, seaweed like in its shape, covers the bark. The trees very often spread their branches into a symmetrical fan shape as though they had been clipped by a landscape gardener. A river in summer is as though made of plates of translucent glass, the top one of which slides. (*PA*, 215)

39. Bell and Marler, *Selected Letters of Vanessa Bell*, 57.

40. See Hussey, *Clive Bell and the Making of Modernism*, 51–80.

41. Bell and Marler, *Selected Letters of Vanessa Bell*, 59.

42. This self-recriminatory line refers to another piece of life writing: Woolf's anonymous contribution to Frederick Maitland's biography of her father, Leslie Stephen, which was published in 1906.

43. As one example, here is a sentence from the 1907 draft (italics mine):

> For the Sacred Monster made you laugh merely to look at *her;* so that you must be a happy person to begin *with* which is a *virtue;* and she so ordered your house and family and servants and love affairs and money and garden and morals, that if you did as she bid *you* you were bound to prosper in this world, and become a *Mayor;* and in the next still brighter *honours* awaited you.

In the revised 1908 typescript, Woolf alters five punctuation marks to give the sentence greater fluidity. She replaces the institutional- or official-sounding word "honours" with "crowns," a more flexible word with literal, figurative, historical, and fanciful associations:

> For the Sacred Monster made you laugh merely to look at ***her,*** so that you must be a happy person to begin ***with,*** which is a ***virtue,*** and she so ordered your house and family and servants and love affairs and money and garden

and morals, that if you did as she bid ***you,*** you were bound to prosper in this world, and become a ***Mayor,*** and in the next still brighter ***crowns*** awaited you.

44. It is unclear when Woolf gave the 1907 typescript to Violet.

45. Lehmann, *Thrown to the Woolfs*, 150–51.

46. Auden, "A Consciousness of Reality," 113.

47. See Maschler, *Publisher*, and Lehmann, *Thrown to the Woolfs*.

48. The Longleat House entry for Woolf's stories has "Friendship's Gallery" with an apostrophe, which is how Violet bound and titled it, but it is not the title as Woolf has it on p. 1 of the story by that name. Both of Violet's penciled notes on the typescript ("1907" and "Typed by Virginia") are erroneous, as this item was professionally typed in 1908.

49. Nor has *The Life of Violet* been included in other collections of Woolf's short stories, such as *Kew Gardens and Other Short Fiction* (ed. Bryony Randall [Oxford University Press, 2022]) or the *Selected Short Stories* (ed. Sandra Kemp [Penguin, 2003/2019]).

50. See Clarke, *The Essays of Virginia Woolf*, vol. 6.

BIBLIOGRAPHY

Auden, W. H. "A Consciousness of Reality." *The New Yorker*. March 6, 1954, 111–16.

Banfield, Ann. *The Phantom Table: Woolf, Fry, Russell and the Epistemology of Modernism*. Cambridge: Cambridge University Press, 2000.

Bell, Vanessa, and Regina Marler. *Selected Letters of Vanessa Bell*. London: Moyer Bell, 1998.

Briggs, Julia. *Reading Virginia Woolf*. Edinburgh: Edinburgh University Press, 2006.

———. *Virginia Woolf: An Inner Life*. New York: Harcourt, 2005.

Burden, Joy. *Winging Westward: From Eton Dungeon to Millfield Desk*. Bath: Robert Wall Books, 1974.

Carlyle, Thomas. *On Heroes, Hero-Worship, and the Heroic in History*. London: James Frazer, 1841.

Clarke, Stuart. Headnote and annotations. Woolf, Virginia, "Friendships Gallery." [1907]. In *The Essays of Virginia Woolf, Volume 6: 1933–1941*, 515–49. London: Hogarth Press, 1979.

Cook, Blanche Wiesen. "'Women Alone Stir My Imagination': Lesbianism and the Cultural Tradition." *Signs: Journal of Women in Culture and Society* 4, no. 4 (1979): 718–39.

Corbett, Mary Jean. *Behind the Times: Virginia Woolf in Late-Victorian Contexts*. Ithaca: Cornell University Press, April 2020.

Curtis, Vanessa, and Julia Briggs. *Virginia Woolf's Women*. Madison: University of Wisconsin Press, 2003.

D'Anethan, Eleanora Mary. *Fourteen Years of Diplomatic Life in Japan: Leaves from the Diary of Baroness Albert d'Anethan*. London: Stanley Paul, 1912.

Dickinson, Violet. [*See Archival Sources below.*]

Eden, Emily. *Miss Eden's Letters Edited by Her Great-Niece Violet Dickinson*. London: Macmillan, 1919.

Forrester, Viviane. *Virginia Woolf: A Portrait*. Translated by Jody Gladding. New York: Columbia University Press, 2015.

Gordon, Lyndall. *Virginia Woolf: A Writer's Life*. New York: W. W. Norton, 1984.

Hawkes, Ellen. Introduction to "Friendships Gallery." *Twentieth Century Literature* 25 (1979): 270–73.

———. "Woolf's 'Magical Garden of Women.'" In *New Feminist Essays on Virginia Woolf*, edited by Jane Marcus. Lincoln: University of Nebraska Press, 1981.

Hussey, Mark. *Clive Bell and the Making of Modernism*. London: Bloomsbury, 2021.

Irvine, Gregory. *Japonisme and the Rise of the Modern Art Movement: The Arts of the Meiji Period*. London: Thames & Hudson, 2013.

King, James. *Virginia Woolf*. New York: W. W. Norton, 1995.

Lee, Hermione. *Virginia Woolf*. New York: Vintage, 1997.

Lehmann, John. *Thrown to the Woolfs: Leonard and Virginia Woolf at the Hogarth Press*. New York: Holt, Rinehart and Winston, 1978.

Lilienfeld, Jane. "'The Gift of a China Inkpot': Violet Dickinson, Virginia Woolf, Elizabeth Gaskell, Charlotte Brontë, and the Love of Women in Writing." In *Virginia Woolf: Lesbian Readings*, edited by Eileen Barrett and Patricia Cramer, 37–56. New York: New York University Press, 1997.

Maschler, Tom. *Publisher*. London: Macmillan, 2007.

McNeillie, Andrew. Introduction to *The Essays of Virginia Woolf: Volume One*. New York: Harcourt Brace Jovanovich, 1986.

Ono, Ayako. *Japonisme in Britain: Whistler, Menpes, Henry, Hornel and Nineteenth-Century Japan*. London: Routledge, 2003.

Rudikoff, Sonya. *Ancestral Houses: Virginia Woolf and the Aristocracy*. Palo Alto Society for Promotion of Science & Scholarship, 1999.

Seshagiri, Urmila. *Race and the Modernist Imagination*. Ithaca: Cornell University Press, 2010.

Simpson, Kathryn. "Friends and Lovers." In *The Oxford Handbook of Virginia Woolf*, edited by Anne E. Fernald, 27–43. Oxford: Oxford University Press, 2021.

Spielmann, Marion Harry, and George Layard. *The Life and Work of Kate Greenaway*. London: Adam and Charles Black, 1905.

Westman, Karin E. "The First Orlando: The Laugh of the Comic Spirit in Virginia Woolf's 'Friendships Gallery.'" *Twentieth Century Literature* 47, no. 1 (2001): 39–71.

Woolf, Virginia. *The Diary of Virginia Woolf*. 5 vols. Edited by Anne Olivier Bell. New York: Harcourt Brace Jovanovich, 1977–85.

———. *The Essays of Virginia Woolf*. Vols. 1–5. Edited by Andrew McNellie. San Diego: Harcourt, 1989–2009.

———. *The Essays of Virginia Woolf: Volume 6: 1933 to 1941*. Edited by Stuart Clarke. London: Hogarth Press, 1979.

———. *The Letters of Virginia Woolf*. 6 vols. Edited by Nigel Nicolson and Joanne Trautmann Banks. New York: Harcourt Brace Jovanovich, 1977–82.

———. "Old Bloomsbury." In *Moments of Being*, edited by Jeanne Schulkind, 181–201. San Diego: Harcourt Brace Jovanovich, 1985.

———. *A Passionate Apprentice*. Edited by Mitchell A. Leaska. London: Hogarth Press, 1990.

———. "Real Letters." *Times Literary Supplement*, Nov. 6, 1919, in *Essays*, vol. 3, 121–23.

———. *A Room of One's Own*. Annotated and introduced by Susan Gubar. Orlando: Harcourt Books, 2005.

———. *Three Guineas*. Edited by Mark Hussey. Annotated and introduced by Jane Marcus. Orlando: Harcourt Books, 2006.

Archival Sources

Captain Humphrey-Davies correspondence, collection of Auckland War Memorial Museum - Tāmaki Paenga Hira. MUS-1995-42-11.

Berg Collection, NYPL. Dickinson, Violet. Album of autographs, photographs, etc., recording world tour, 1905. 36 cm. 1 v. with compiler's holograph notes.

Berg Collection, NYPL. Friendships [G]allery. Typescript with ms. corrections in the author's and unidentified hands. "Written by Virginia Stephen and typed by her in 1907" is penciled in on p. [1] by Violet Dickinson. Bound. Includes her "A Story to Make You Sleep" [36–52], n.d., 52 pages, typescripts (emended).

Longleat House. Woolf, Virginia, 1882–1941. "Friendship's Gallery" [Longleat typescript]. Friendship's Gallery [Chapter I], The Magic Garden [Chapter II], A Story to Make You Sleep [Chapter III]. f f.47. Unpublished carbon typescript, 1907. Inscription: Marked by Violet Dickinson in pencil "1907" and "Typed by Virginia."

Somerset Heritage Centre. "Mary Violet Dickinson; 9th Generation." *Manuscript History of the Dickinson Family*, vol. 2, 1940. DD/DN/5/6/3 (pp. 116–27).

———. Typescript manuscript of *God's Protecting Providence by Jonathan Dickinson, with a preface by his kinswoman Violet Dickinson*, ca. 1930s. DD/DN/5/5/3 (1–17).

University of Sussex Library. *Early Writings by Virginia Woolf*, in *Monks House Papers: Papers of Virginia Woolf and Related Papers of Leonard Woolf*. Reference no. SxMs18-2-A-26 (pp. 73–78). Diary entry 1902.

Unpublished items from the Violet Dickinson Collection, Longleat.

Washington State University. Harte, Anthony. *These Thoughts Were Written By Anthony Harte*. S. l.: s. n., 1905. VW—presentee. Violet Dickinson—inscriber.

INDEX

Not included: Violet Dickinson, Virginia Woolf, works by Virginia Woolf

A NOTE ON THE TYPE

This book has been composed in Arno, an Old-style serif typeface in the classic Venetian tradition, designed by Robert Slimbach at Adobe.